MURDER AT THE DOCTOR'S OFFICE

Book Two

Joe McCullen Cozy Mystery Series

Tanya R. Taylor

D1713800

**Never Miss a New Release by
Tanya R. Taylor!**

GET BOOK THREE IN THIS EXCITING, NEW COZY MYSTERY SERIES!

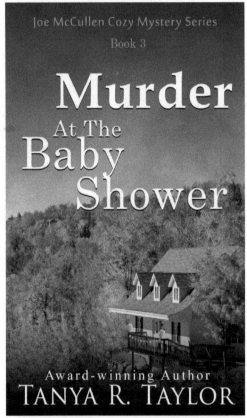

Joe McCullen Cozy Mystery Series

Book 3

Murder
At The
Baby
Shower

Award-winning Author
TANYA R. TAYLOR

VISIT TANYA-R-TAYLOR.COM

"You said you would help us!" Todd Robinson looked angrily into the eyes of the man he once thought was their savior. "But now after you've butchered my wife and taken nearly every dime we had you claim there's nothing more that you can do?"

Dr. Mark Bridges remained composed despite the man's ranting. The Robinsons were seated in his spacious office on the other side of the desk.

"You both knew what we were facing here," Bridges said. "I explained to you from the day you walked through that door that I would do whatever I could to help and I kept my word."

Sitting quietly in her wheelchair next to her husband, Melanie Robinson was just a shell of the person she was when she first walked through the main door of Dr. Bridges' private practice some six months earlier. Since then, she'd lost forty pounds, was in constant pain and depended on a portable ventilator in order to breathe.

"That's a lie and you know it!" Todd countered. "You convinced us that if she had that surgery you went on about, all of her pain would go away. But none of it was true. Instead, having the surgery made her condition a thousand times worse! She would've been better off if we'd just left everything alone."

"That was a choice you both made and now you sit here and blame me for it? Your wife signed a document stating that she was aware of all the risks involved and would not hold this office responsible. Now—since things didn't turn out the way we hoped they would, you're acting the fool—as if you had no idea what could happen? I find that truly amazing."

Melanie was sobbing and shaking her head weakly in protest. She could no longer speak since he removed a small abnormal growth from her mouth. Todd reached for her frail hand and gently squeezed it.

"I am willing to keep her medicated until…that time comes…to ensure that she's as comfortable as possible," Bridges said. "But aside from that, there's nothing more that I can do. There's nothing more that anybody can do."

Todd stared at him as if he'd given his wife, the love of his life, a death sentence and it felt like every bit of strength inside him had left. Yet, he was hearing it from Dr. Bridges for the second time and the sound of it was no easier to bear.

Mark Bridges was an ENT surgeon with more degrees behind his name than a thermometer. He'd worked at the local hospital fresh out of medical school and a few days out of the week for two private clinics. At age twenty-eight, after he'd tied the knot with his college sweetheart Camila, he started his own private practice and in less than a year became a multimillionaire.

Todd stood up and positioned himself at the handles of his wife's wheelchair. "Let's go, honey," he said.

Bridges didn't bother to get up as they were leaving. Then at the door, Todd turned and looked at him while keeping a supportive hand on Melanie.

"I am a man of faith, Doctor, and I promise you that you will reap what you've sown. You will pay for what you did to my wife and so will those two children you love so much. Mark my words."

At the mention of his children, Bridges abruptly stood up and glared at him, but he didn't say a word.

As the Robinsons slowly proceeded through the main office, they passed Dr. Bridges' assistant, Cherry, whose desk was situated right outside his door, and a few patients waiting to be seen.

Cherry's heart went out to them as she'd seen them faithfully show up for appointments almost every week for months. However, as chatty as she usually was with them, she wasn't sure of what to say to them that day as they were leaving. Feeling awkward about it and sensing that it would probably be their last time at the office, she said nothing.

Cherry Granger, a slender brunette, had been a faithful employee of Dr. Mark Bridges for nineteen years. She'd answered an ad for an assistant job just after she'd graduated high school that spring of 1999—the year he'd opened the doors of his private practice for the first time. She was the longest serving employee and had climbed the ranks with extra duties such as hiring and overseeing the running of the office. Her career had taken precedence over any romantic interests, and now that she was of the impression that childbearing wasn't in the cards for her, she still had no regrets. Rather, she looked forward to the next chapter of her life which involved moving into the small cottage she'd recently purchased near the sea, spending countless hours daily in a hammock in the back yard, and sipping coconut water right out of the shell. In two weeks, she would be retiring to the Cayman Islands where she intended to live out the rest of her days, single, free and leaving the hustle and bustle of Old Providence far behind.

Thirty-year-old Heather Caddel, a new employee of only five months, who took care of all the coding for insurance purposes as well as cashing duties, had replaced Beulah Hart who'd left to pursue a degree full-time in accounting—her first love. Beulah had been in Dr. Bridges' employ for ten years and had built a good life within that timeframe with the help of an average salary. She had three children and a supportive husband who worked long hours as a truck driver. The aspiring accountant had never lost touch with Cherry since the two, over the years, had forged an inseparable bond.

Cherry got up and hurried into Bridges' office. He was seated at his desk, sliding aside Melanie's file.

"Is everything all right, sir?" she asked. "The Robinsons seemed highly upset."

"Everything's perfect!" he replied, interlacing his fingers and giving them a good crack. "Send in the next patient please."

"Sure!" Cherry nodded.

The commotion at the office that morning had not been a solitary event. Cherry had witnessed several patients over the years confront her boss for what they deemed was subpar and, at times, inhumane service, though some chose to use certain ear-jarring expletives within those walls to express the same sentiment. However, the Robinsons' case appeared more extreme to her. She'd never seen another patient of his deteriorate so quickly and the pain she'd seen in Todd Robinson's eyes due to his wife's suffering was indelible.

She promptly went over to Oria Zervous, a seventy-four-year-old Scottish lady who'd been waiting to see Dr. Bridges for the better part of an hour. She'd been visiting the office faithfully for a few weeks due to her sinus issues.

"Doctor Bridges will see you now," Cherry told her.

"It's about time!" Oria snarled. "I keep telling you people that I do have a life, you know."

She fixed her purse on her wrinkled foreman and slowly marched toward Dr. Bridge's office.

Cherry returned to her desk and resumed her work. That's when Heather walked over.

"Just two more weeks and you'll be the envy of all you're leaving behind," Heather said.

"I'm counting down the days."

"I don't need to ask if you're eager about retirement."

Cherry looked at her. "No, you don't!"

"I feel really sorry for the Robinsons." Heather lowered her voice almost to a whisper.

"I do too. They're such a nice couple."

"Do you think Mrs. Robinson's gonna be okay?"

Cherry sighed. "You know I'm an optimist, Heather, but based on how quickly she seems to be declining, I truly believe only a miracle can save her now. She was so vibrant when she first came here. Such a pleasant lady who always kept a smile on her face."

"What a difference now, huh?" She sadly shook her head.

"Yep. Seems like life just knocked the wind right out of her."

"Either life—or Doctor Bridges," Heather replied before walking off.

* * * *

"It's okay, honey," Todd told his wife. "Let's get you into bed now."

He locked the wheels of her chair and gently lifted her onto their bed.

"Do you want me to pull the covers up for you?"

Melanie shook her head.

Todd could see the sadness in her eyes and had spent countless nights praying that somehow he could take her place and she could be well again. But his prayers went unanswered.

"Don't worry about that jerk!" he said. "His time will come."

She turned her head to the right against the pillow, looking at him and wondering how she'd ended up that way.

Todd knelt beside her and held her hand. "Honey, I want you to know that none of this is your fault. I don't want you blaming yourself for going to a doctor who you thought could help. Never mind what I said and what I thought.

13

None of us could've predicted what was going to happen. Okay?"

She nodded.

He kissed her hand and stood up. "I'm gonna go make lunch. Be right back."

Immediately, she reached over to the nightstand for the little pad and pen she kept on hand.

Todd waited while she scribbled something. Then she held it up.

He smiled widely. "I love you too, honey."

2

---

ight days later...

The parish's annual fair was a highly anticipated event. Particularly during the last four months leading up to the big day, Father Joe McCullen was often energetically making plans to ensure the fair would be a huge success and a fun time for parishioners.

Balloons attached to tents on the church grounds could be spotted from the main road that Saturday as scores of people filled the yard, finding themselves involved in one curious event or the other. Tammy Li and her eleven-year-old triplets were at the hoopla booth as Dora, the eldest by two minutes, took her turn trying to get the ring around the large, brown teddy bear.

"It's my turn!" Joe heard Sally, the youngest of the Li children exclaim. Her mother quickly paid for another colorful ring and handed it to the eager little girl.

Sitting at a table with his secretary, Sue McCloud, and sipping on punch, Joe was smiling inside as he observed the families gather for their special time together. Reflecting upon his own childhood, he recalled the many happy times he and his brothers, Ed and Charlie, and sister, Breanne, spent each year attending the annual diocesan fair with their mother, Matilda. Their mother never missed a church fair, but his father, Lawrence, wasn't much of a churchgoer to begin with, so he was hardly interested in any church activities either. His parents were polar opposites, but despite that Joe and his siblings enjoyed a quiet, peaceful childhood. Somehow, the adults managed to make things work.

Dressed in a cotton white collared shirt and black slacks, Joe got up and headed over to the DJ a few feet away.

"Ready?" he asked.

Francois gave the priest a nod and immediately went to retrieve the record.

"Okay…it's party time!" Joe announced, making his way over to a large area near the bouncing castle that was sectioned off with blue tape. Mike Tenney and a fellow altar boy, Rich Dalton, quickly removed a portion of the tape and Joe walked over to the center of the pavement. Just then, the Electric Boogie song came on and dozens of people joined Joe on the pavement. Sue being the first to get there and others gathering around to watch.

Mike and Rich looked on as Father Joe and others, young and old, moved to the beat of the song, not missing a step. Tammy Li and her triplets joined in and the girls were keeping up with the turns better than their mom.

"I've got to move…I'm going on a party ride…" Joe sang happily as he moved two steps back again with an obvious pep in his step.

Mike was grinning. Rich Dalton, next to him, thought Joe looked like an overly inflated Santa on the dance floor and had laughed himself to tears. For the past few years, he'd watched his priest get out there and lead the popular dance with belly protruding and all, and each time, it tickled the teenager just the same. Virginia Adams and Kate Brown, who both worked at the church, were standing near the front holding their soft drinks.

"Every year, without fail, he makes a fool of himself," Virginia said, shaking her head.

Kate smiled. "Father Joe is one of a kind. Surely, the life of the party."

"He's a priest, for crying out loud! What happened to sanctity, holiness and all that other stuff?"

"Just because he's dancing makes him unholy and unsanctified?" Kate grimaced. "It's not a sin, you know."

"How do you know?" Virginia replied. "If it isn't a sin for anyone else, I'm almost certain it is for him."

Kate was inching closer to the pavement and Virginia followed.

"Hold this!" Kate finally handed Virginia her soft drink and she hurried toward the dancers.

"Hey, where are you going?" Virginia cried.

"Where does it look like?"

Kate quickly caught up with the dance and was having herself a blast.

Virginia sucked her teeth and glanced around. Other onlookers were smiling, laughing and chatting away.

"If these people call this entertainment, they need to get out more," she muttered.

After the dance, Joe made his way over to the main door of the church office to use the restroom. Agatha Hall, the office administrator, met him at the door.

"Hey, Agatha. What are you doing cooped up in here when all the fun's outside?" he asked.

"I was just coming to find you, Father," she said, anxiously.

"What is it?" He soon noticed the look of concern on her face.

"It's Melanie Robinson. Her husband Todd just called to say she's at the very end, I'm afraid. He asks that you please come over right away to administer last rites to her."

"Well, I'm sorry to hear that," he replied, sadly. "Will do."

Joe continued on to the restroom, then hurried over to the rectory to retrieve the items needed to help Melanie with her inevitable demise. He brought along his coat and clerical collar and headed to the car.

As he drove, he thought about the Robinsons and how Melanie had been faithful in attending Mass before she got sick. Todd, on the other hand, had shown up to church maybe once or twice within the last three years to his recollection. Joe didn't know him very well, but could tell that the couple had a loving relationship. The last time he'd seen Melanie was just a week earlier after he'd stopped by the house to check on her as he'd been doing in recent months.

You need to slow down, he recalled her last words to him before she could no longer speak. Her voice just prior to that had been weak and soft, almost to a whisper. She'd been having terrible headaches that were barely responding to the strongest medication she'd been prescribed.

Joe sighed deeply. "Lord, be with her," he uttered, feeling the weight of sorrow in his heart. Melanie had just turned forty-eight three months earlier and in his mind, she was still so young to be facing death.

Administering the last rites was never an easy task for the priest although he'd been at it numerous times over the course of many years. Looking into a person's eyes as they faced the grim reality that death was very near, and doing what it took in his capacity to assist in ensuring that their transition from this earth would be seamless was never something he looked forward to. He could clearly recall the day after his fifteenth birthday when Father John Giosi had entered his childhood home to administer last rites to his mother and how lost he'd felt. Although he was eternally grateful to the priest for his selfless act of consolation, he could never forget how final it felt, as if all hope for his mother had vanished forever. And it did. She passed away within hours of receiving the priest's blessing.

Joe pulled up in front of the Robinsons' driveway. Melanie's silver sedan was parked on the right side and Todd's white van he'd recently purchased with the wheelchair support ramp stood on the left near the door. Todd's truck was in front of the house, a few yards from where Joe had parked.

Todd was a contractor by trade and had built a comfortable, two thousand square foot home for his wife of the past fourteen years. How he felt about her was no secret to those who knew them. He practically worshipped the ground she walked on.

Joe could only imagine the intense emotional pain the man was feeling knowing that at any moment, Melanie would breathe her last breath, leaving him all alone in the house they'd shared.

Reaching for his Bible and Holy oil, Joe stepped out of the car and used his alarm key to lock it. As he headed for the front porch of the lovely single-story yellow house, Todd opened the front door and walked hastily toward the priest. The men met halfway along the narrow, concrete walkway.

"Thank you for coming, Father," Todd said in a lowered voice.

Joe could see that he'd been crying. "How is she—emotionally, that is?" he asked.

"She's at peace with the fact that she'll soon be gone. She's been having a hard time breathing, but refuses to go back to the hospital. I must respect her final wishes, Father. She's been through so much."

"I understand." Joe patted his back. "Take me to her."

Joe followed Todd into the house, shutting the door behind them. Then they took a quick left just off the hallway into the couple's bedroom. Melanie was lying on the bed, frail and nearly lifeless with a feeding tube attached, but her breathing was obviously labored. The sound of it was nerve-racking and Joe was almost tempted to ask Todd if he was sure about not calling an ambulance for her. Yet, he knew the couple's struggles and was aware that Melanie had been admitted repeatedly in recent weeks for the same complaint, each time plummeting her deeper into depression. Doctors in the emergency room, along with her own doctor had made it clear that there was nothing more they could do for her.

"Melanie…" Joe walked up to her bedside. "It's me—Father Joe."

Melanie nodded twice.

Joe reached for her hand. "Do you know why I'm here today?" he asked.

Again, this time with her eyes brimming with tears, she nodded.

"Is it your decision not to go back to the hospital?" He felt compelled to ask.

She nodded again.

Joe glanced at Todd who was struggling to restrain the tears welling in his eyes, then he turned to Melanie again.

"I want you to know, dear, that you are not alone. The angels are here with you and will help you along your journey. Death, with all its mystery, is a remarkable event for those who know the wondrous life that awaits them on the other side. Rest assured that God has you covered and is ready to welcome you home with open arms when that time comes."

With a tear streaming down her face, Melanie weakly nodded.

"And don't you worry about Todd here. He'll be just fine. I plan to keep an eye on him and make sure he gets to Mass more often."

She managed a slight smile.

Joe commenced the ritual which began with him making the sign of the cross. He then proceeded to recite special prayers for the benefit of the dying which, by Melanie's expression, appeared to give her some level of comfort. Lastly, Joe anointed her forehead and her hands with holy oil. He soon realized that her breathing had quieted down to a degree, seeming less labored and he was hoping it was a good sign that miraculously, she'd pull through.

Before leaving her bedside for what might be the final time, he gave Melanie some parting words of comfort and she gently squeezed his hand. When she did that, in his heart, he was certain that it would be his last time seeing her alive. Minutes before his mother died, she did the same thing and since her passing, he took it as a clear indicator of a person's near departure and their final gesture of love.

"I want to thank you wholeheartedly for coming out for Melanie," Todd said as he walked with Joe to his car.

"I must confess it's never easy for me," Joe told him. "Especially when it's someone like Melanie that I've known for a long time."

Todd sighed.

"You know I'm here for you if you ever need someone to talk to, Todd. I realize this is an incredibly difficult time in your life, but God will help you through it. You're not alone either."

"I appreciate that, Father."

The men shook hands.

"Drive safely, Father," Todd said as Joe fastened his seatbelt.

"I will. God bless you both."

That night at 7:55 P.M., Joe received a call from Todd that Melanie had passed away. He said that her final moments were peaceful.

<u>3</u>

"I heard about Melanie," Sue McCloud told Agatha at work the following Monday morning. "I'm very sorry. I know you were close to the couple."

"I am," Agatha replied, sadly. "Thankfully, I got to say goodbye to her just in time. "It's like she waited until I'd left to pass on. I hadn't opened the screen door to my house good before Todd called with the awful news."

Sue felt her sorrow and tried to console her as the tears streamed down her face.

"She was one of my best friends," Agatha said. "No one could have asked for a better friend than she was. She had a good life though. Todd had seen to that."

"I know."

"I have no idea what he's going to do now; he looked so lost after she'd died. There was no consoling him." She dried her tears with a tissue. "He blames that Doctor Bridges for what happened to Melanie and I personally have to agree with him. The man's a butcher. The way he handled her after the botch job he'd done was horrendous. The arrogant son of a gun couldn't care less that he'd ruined her health and her life. I just don't understand it!"

"God doesn't sleep, Agatha. Some people you just don't mess with in this world because then His judgment comes quickly."

"I agree." Agatha blew her nose. That fool's gonna cross the wrong one someday. I'm sure of it."

* * * *

"I can't believe you're leaving us!" Heather told Cherry as they sat in the kitchen before the office opened for business.

Cherry sighed. "I've worked long enough and since it's only been me, I've been able to save up to go on early retirement. It's my time now to relax and enjoy what's left of my life."

She was wearing a sunny sleeveless dress that hung a couple of inches below her knees and was feeling quite vibrant that day with all things considered.

"What's left of your life, you say. You act as if you're old and decrepit, Cherry!" Heather exclaimed. "You could've put in more time if you wanted and grown an even better nest egg."

"That's the key..." Cherry pointed out. "*If* I wanted. The fact is I don't. Why are you so anti-retirement?"

"I'm not!" Heather giggled. "The truth is...I just got here less than six months ago and after having warmed up to you, you're leaving in like four days. You're the life of this place and now you're moving on."

Smiling, Cherry took a sip of her black coffee. "Thanks, Heather. That's very kind of you, but in my view, you're the one who lights up this office. You always have a smile on your face no matter what you may be going through. And it's been an inspiration for me to have a more positive outlook and appreciate each day, regardless of what it brings."

"Really?" Heather searched her eyes.

"Is that so hard to believe?" Cherry asked.

Heather was slowly stirring her coffee with the metal spoon she'd left inside of the mug. "It's just that I don't think anyone has ever said something as nice to me before."

"Well, it's the truth! As far as I'm concerned, you're that special of a person."

"Thank you, Cherry." Heather smiled. "Lord knows this office can use as many good vibes as it can possibly get, especially with all the complaints we've been getting. And that Mrs. Bridges… what a snob! Whenever she comes in here, she acts like we're the dirt under her shoes. The woman doesn't even say hello! Just boldly asks for her husband."

"I'm so used to it." Cherry sighed. "None of it even bothers me anymore. Over the years, I just came to accept that people will be who they are and I can't change anyone. So, why try? I'm not getting high blood pressure over someone's nasty behavior."

Just then, Dr. Bridges entered the room.

"Good morning, ladies!" he said, quite happily as he headed over to the coffee pot.

"Good morning, Doctor," they replied.

"Well, you seem to be in a cheerful mood this morning!" Cherry told him.

"I'm always in a cheerful mood. Haven't you noticed?" He retrieved his mug from the cupboard, then poured out some coffee.

Cherry and Heather glanced at each other as if Bridges had posed a trick question.

"Well, Cherry?" He sauntered over to the table.

"I guess," she answered.

Heather lowered her head and took another sip of her coffee, hoping he wouldn't ask her opinion.

"You guess? Aww…I thought I'd made a better impression over all these years. Guess I'd have to do a better job in the days you have left, huh?"

Cherry smiled.

"What about you, Heather?" He asked.

"Sir?" Heather looked up at him, feeling awkward.

"Haven't you noticed that I'm always in a good mood? Maybe Cherry just turned a blind eye to it for some reason or the other."

Heather desperately wanted to be truthful, especially since she viewed him as an extremely egotistical and arrogant man.

"Yes, you're always in a cheerful mood, sir," she replied.

Cherry glanced at her, making no judgments.

"See, Cherry?" Bridges shook his head with a smug look on his face. "Heather's noticed. Maybe you just weren't paying attention."

"I guess I wasn't," Cherry replied.

Checking his watch while heading for the door, he said, "We'll be open soon, so don't let your coffee get cold."

Heather and Cherry looked at each other.

"Can you believe that man?" Heather said, quietly. "He's nothing more than a bully, if you ask me."

"He's our boss," Cherry replied. "I told you from the beginning that he had his ways and if you were going to have a career here, you'd have to accept them. It's as simple as that, Heather. I've taken my own advice over the past nineteen years and so should you.

Heather was quiet.

Cherry patted the top of her hand. "You'll be just fine. Doctor Bridges has his really kind moments too."

"Girl…I am gonna miss you."

"Drink up!" Cherry smiled. "We'll be open in ten minutes."

Without another word, they both focused on finishing their coffee.

4

---

*F*our days later…

Funeral services for Melanie Robinson were being held that Friday morning. The organist played a well-known hymn as people streamed in one by one viewing Melanie's body in the foyer.

Before long, the church was packed to capacity; most of those in attendance were fellow parishioners who'd come to know and love her. Her parents, Albert and Cleo Witticker were seated up front with Todd, along with Melanie's younger sister, Tonya. Todd's brother Clark sitting to his left, had flown in from Tulsa with his wife and three children.

Brook Spade, a twenty-two-year-old member of the youth choir took to the microphone and presented a stunning rendition of one of Melanie's favorite songs: 'It is well with my soul'. Todd broke down in tears and Clark quickly wrapped his arm around his brother's shoulder and held him. Melanie's parents and sister were all drenched in tears after the first verse had been beautifully rendered. Agatha, seated directly behind Todd, looked toward the aisle as church attendants, walking slowly, gently rolled her friend's casket toward the center of the church. She couldn't help noticing how much honor the men displayed for her beloved friend and she began to weep. The casket was of a rose gold finish with white interior. Melanie had been dressed in an eloquent royal blue gown she'd worn a year earlier at her sister-in-law's wedding and her hair had been stylishly pinned up with long curls dangling on both sides of her narrow face. Agatha had thought she looked angelic and all signs of the previous distress she'd suffered in her body prior to her demise appeared to have vanished from her face. Agatha reached forward and gently touched Todd's shoulder as he wept bitterly for his wife. She'd seen when he glanced behind, realizing the casket was now closed and it was the last time anyone would ever see her again. The moment, for Agatha, felt unnervingly final and she could only imagine what that meant for Todd.

By the time Brook had stepped off the podium, most of the congregation were drenched in tears.

Soon Tonya Manilow, Melanie's sister, went up and spoke lovingly about the woman she described as one having undaunting courage and strength. "She left us way too soon," she cried. "What I've been trying to figure out since the moment she passed is how am I supposed to live without my sister!"

Looking on, Father Joe felt her undeniable distress which even brought tears to his eyes. However, he quickly sought to compose himself since he knew others were relying on him to be a source of strength. After a while, he came forward with the homily which included words of encouragement and consolation, particularly for Melanie's family.

"Can you believe he only invited their people to take holy communion? It's a slap in the face!" Terecita Lathglow, a longtime friend of Melanie's parents said to her daughter Nadia in the parking lot after the funeral. "Wait 'til my pastor hears about this."

Shaking her head, Nadia replied, "Mom, must you always nitpick? We are not members and must respect the church's rules whether we agree with them or not. For instance—no one is allowed to wear makeup or jewelry at your church—as ludicrous as that seems to me. So, Pastor Nate nor anyone else in authority there has the right to criticize any other church for its rules and regulations."

Sucking her teeth, Terecita hurried toward their car, leaving her daughter behind to catch up.

* * * *

Cherry was seated at her desk smiling at the large, rectangular pound cake with pineapple filling in the middle and pink and white icing on top. Dr. Bridges, Heather and Nurse June Mortimer were all standing around her.

That afternoon after the office had closed for business, Heather carried the large cake as the others quickly followed her to Cherry's desk. Cherry, caught by surprise, was speechless.

"We wish you a wonderful retirement, Cherry, and we'll miss you around here," Heather said.

"We surely will," June added, rubbing Cherry's back.

June Mortimer had been in Dr. Bridges' employ for eleven years and was now in her early sixties. She was like a mother figure to the women in the office and also a good friend of the Bridges.

"I...I don't know what to say," Cherry finally said with tears in her eyes.

"Say Bon Voyage!" Bridges exclaimed.

And everyone laughed.

"Seriously—" he continued, moving in closer to her desk. "Cherry, I don't need to tell you what you mean to me and my practice. We've been two peas in a pod since right after I opened these doors for business for the very first time almost twenty years ago. We've helped a lot of people and I noticed from the beginning that you always had a special way of dealing with clients—making them feel welcome and as a part of our family here. Gosh! I'm so used to depending on you for practically everything, knowing you'd get the job done." He sighed heavily. "It's gonna take quite a bit of getting used to the fact that you're not gonna be here anymore to help me with anything. I'm gonna really miss you, Cherry."

"Aww..." June interlaced her fingers.

Cherry looked at her boss, almost feeling guilty about her decision to leave. "That's so sweet of you, Doctor Bridges. I will surely miss being here too. This office has been a big part of my life for practically all of my adult life. So, I'm sure that not coming here anymore is going to take some getting used to as well," she said.

"Oh! Enough of all the doom and gloom. Let's cut the cake!" June said. "Heather, turn on the music. Let's get this party officially started!"

Heather hurried over to the tape player she'd brought from home and June dashed into the kitchen to grab the paper plates and forks.

* * * *

That night, Bridges stayed late at the office to catch up on reports and read test results as he did most weeknights. Everyone had left after the party and he'd seen Cherry Granger off with an envelope bearing a fairly large check for her years of service.

As he sat in his office working, the little hand on the clock attached above his door struck half past seven and he heard a sound some distance away near the corridor.

Just one other light was on in the front section of the building.

"Is anyone there?" he cried, glancing up at the clock.

"Maybe it's the cleaners," he muttered, before resuming his work.

A few minutes sailed by, then from his peripheral vision, he thought he spotted something in the doorway. Looking up, his eyes widened as he saw someone standing there pointing a gun in his direction.

"What? What are you…"

"Your reign of terror ends tonight," the person frankly stated. "I'm here to see to it."

And the gun went off.

5

The following day…

With her purse strapped to her shoulder, Agatha hurried up the walkway toward the front porch.

She pressed the doorbell repeatedly and moments later, the door swung open.

"Agatha…" Todd said. "I wasn't expecting you."

He was wearing an old tee shirt and baggy blue jeans, and his hair was ruffled.

"Can I come in?" she asked.

"You never needed an invitation before."

"Yeah. You're right." She walked in and shut the door behind her.

Todd took a seat on the couch and Agatha sat across from him.

"Have you heard the news?" she asked. "Honestly, I couldn't get here fast enough. Came right after work."

Agatha worked at the church on Saturdays until noon.

"I haven't been listening to any news." Todd sighed. "Been sleeping all morning."

She positioned herself at the edge of her seat. "Mel's butcher of a doctor was found in his office with a bullet to the forehead last night."

Todd sat back silently.

"Did you hear what I said?"

"Yeah. Serves him right."

Agatha expected a more dramatic response.

"Isn't that something?" she continued. "He finally crossed the wrong one and probably faced death a lot sooner than expected. And I doubt he ever imagined the way he'd go." She leaned back and crossed her legs. "I must admit, I don't feel an ounce of remorse for him or his family. The way he treated Mel was atrocious. He should've been put in front of a firing squad as far as I'm concerned. That would've served him right."

"Do they know who did it?" Todd folded his arms.

"Doesn't sound so. I guess it's too early in the investigation to know."

43

He nodded.

After a few moments of silence, she asked, "How are you doing?"

Todd looked at her intently. "How do you think I'm doing? Mel's dead. Remember?"

"I'm sorry. I just…"

"Don't apologize." He quickly shook his head. "That was rude of me, Agatha. You didn't deserve that."

"So, Mel's parents. Are they still…"

"Nah. They took off right after the funeral. There's nothing for them to stick around here for since Mel's gone."

He cupped his face with his hands and Agatha immediately got up and went to him.

She sat down and reached for his hand. "Todd, I want you to know that I'm always here for you. Only a phone call away if you ever need anything—even if it's just someone to talk to."

"Thanks, Agatha. You were always here for us. I wouldn't expect any different."

She looked around the house and everything reminded her of Melanie. Her pictures on the living room wall; her yellow scarf thrown across the arm of the sofa; the scent of her perfume collection she kept on a stand near the bedroom door. Mel designed the interior of their house. It was her touch that gave the place a warm, cozy feel.

"It's going to take some time to get used to the fact that she isn't here anymore, Todd. But I do believe the pain associated with her loss will begin to soften in time. And in the meanwhile, my best friend would want you to live. Yes—grieve for as long as you must. But remember to honor her wishes with respect to what she would've totally wanted for you—which is to take care of yourself and to not allow yourself to sink so deeply into despair." She quickly released his hand. "Maybe I shouldn't be saying all of this right now since the wound is still so fresh."

Todd's face softened a bit as he looked at her. "I understand what you mean."

"Okay, good." She smiled.

She stood up slowly. "Well, I'd better let you get back to your rest."

Todd stood as well. "Thanks for coming by and letting me know about that jerk," he said. "Also—for the words of encouragement. I really appreciate it, even though we got off to a rough start."

"I know you appreciate it." Agatha smiled. "And I'd be heartless to take offence, knowing what you're going through right now."

He shoved his hands into his pockets.

"Well, I'll see you later. And remember…I'm only a phone call away."

She walked out and headed to her car.

* * * *

Cherry went around the western side of the old cottage she'd purchased and attempted to adjust the shutter that was leaning slightly. She'd caught the flight to Grand Cayman the day before and was eager to get settled into her new place.

Cayman was where she'd spent most of her childhood years until she was sent to live in Old Providence with her grandaunt, Karen, who was disabled and needed the help. Cherry spent her senior year in school there, graduating two weeks after Karen passed away.

Now, she was home again where her heart had always been. And although she loved her relatives and had made it a point to visit them on the island every year, being particular about privacy and knowing they would have a hard time respecting that, she opted for a small home a long drive away from all of them.

Her Uncle Steve had a pub he'd left for her two years earlier that she'd allowed his trusted friend Julio to continue to run. They'd made an arrangement that he would deposit the profits of the business into her personal bank account faithfully every month after salaries and other expenses were deducted. Undoubtedly, it had helped her reach her goal of early retirement a little sooner than she'd initially anticipated.

"This darn thing!" She muttered as the shutter kept slipping out of place. "Guess fixing this small problem will be my first expense." She sighed.

"Hi there!" A woman hailed her from a good way off.

"Hi!" Cherry hailed back. The closest house was a hundred yards from hers which she felt wasn't too bad.

She proceeded around the house under the shade of tall coconut and palm trees. The backyard of the cottage led out to the sea and

Cherry smiled as she looked out at the clear blue water glistening in the sun.

"This is Heaven," she said, opening the gate, then walking onto the beach.

There were only a few persons out on the stretch as far as she could see and she proceeded to remove her slippers and get her feet wet. The water was cold although the weather that day was quite sunny. But she didn't care. This is what she wanted; it was what she'd longed for.

Just then, her cell phone vibrated in her pocket and she quickly retrieved it.

"Cherry, it's me…Beulah."

"Hey, Beulah! Checking up on me already?" She smiled.

"I have bad news. It's Doctor Bridges…"

"What about him?"

"He's…dead."

"What?" Cherry exclaimed. "What do you mean he's dead? How? He was fine yesterday."

"Someone killed him at the office."

"Oh, no!"

"No one there contacted you about this? I was trying to reach you all morning, but kept getting your voicemail," Beulah said.

"I forgot that my phone was on vibrate. I just slipped it into my pocket before I came outside and that's how come I got this call. I'd have to check my messages in case someone from the office was trying to reach me about it. But this is all so disturbing!"

"I'd say!"

"Do they have the killer in custody?" Cherry asked.

"Not yet. They're asking for assistance from the public in the case. I wonder who could've done something like this. The man had his faults, but he didn't deserve to die."

"I really wonder where they'd start in terms of a suspect," Cherry replied. "Doctor Bridges had made a number of patients quite angry over the years."

"You're telling me? I used to work there, remember?"

"Yep. I'm just so shocked by this. I can't believe we're having this conversation. Seems surreal."

"I'm sorry, hun. I know this affects you more than it does any other employee of his since you've worked with him the longest."

"I'd better check my messages now." Cherry sighed. "Thanks for letting me know, Beulah."

She ended the call.

6

Heather watched stoically from a chair in the lobby as police transported boxes of files they retrieved from Dr. Bridges' office inside the station. Camila Bridges and Nurse June Mortimer were both present in small rooms assisting the police.

"Are you all right?" A male officer asked Heather.

"Yes, I'm fine." She glanced up at him.

"Detective Jackson will have a word with you shortly."

"Okay." Heather nodded.

Detective Sam Jackson sat across the desk from Camila who was sobbing.

"I can't believe my husband's been murdered," she cried. "And that you've already ransacked his office!"

"We're just doing what must be done in order to find out who is responsible for your husband's death, Mrs. Bridges," Jackson told her.

"Did you have to tear the place apart like that? June and the other girl out there could've gathered the files for you and handed them over instead of you all destroying everything Mark has spent his life trying to build!"

"I hardly believe collecting files is destroying what your husband has built, ma'am."

"I'm not interested in your belief, Detective!" The sobbing abruptly stopped. "I know what I've seen with my own eyes and your officers wouldn't even allow me to get past the door of the building."

"That's because it's officially a crime scene. We're trying to preserve evidence," he explained. "Now, can you please answer the question I asked you earlier?"

"What's that?" She grimaced.

"To the best of your knowledge, did your husband have any enemies?"

She threw a hand up. "You mean—other than his brother Ted who accused him a year ago of stealing his share of the investment deal?"

"What investment?" Jackson asked, curiously.

"Some stock market thing they both put money into. Mark used his broker to do the deal and Ted had no objections. Next thing you know, a couple of years down the line Ted accused Mark of stealing the money. But it was lost because the startup they'd invested in collapsed. It's that simple! Ted just didn't seem to understand. He surely wasn't the brightest of the bunch in the Bridges family, so it's kind of understandable that he couldn't possibly comprehend a simple explanation as that."

"So, Ted was really upset?"

"*Upset* isn't the word!" Camila replied. "He promised he'd get Mark back for outsmarting him, but until last night, I didn't know he'd despised his brother so much."

Jackson requested Ted's full name and contact information.

"Is there anyone else you can think of who might've had it in for your husband, Mrs. Bridges?"

She leaned back and sighed. "My husband was an excellent surgeon who helped countless people in this community and gave them a better quality of life. However, as you know, Detective, you can't please everybody regardless of how hard you try…"

"I'm aware of that." Jackson slowly nodded.

"With that said, there a few people over the years who fit into the category of *hard to please*."

"Do you know their names?"

"I don't, but I'm sure his staff would be of greater assistance in that regard."

Jackson turned the page of his yellow legal pad. "Where did you say you were between the hours of 7:00 and 9:00 P.M.?" he asked.

"You asked me that last night, when you and some lady officer…showed up on my doorstep to tell me my husband was killed. Remember?"

"Detective Kenna…"

"Who? What?"

"That's who accompanied me last night to your home," he stated.

"Yeah. Well, I told you that I was at a friend's birthday party. A good many people can verify that I was there at least until eleven-thirty."

Jackson glanced down at his notes. He hadn't forgotten what she'd stated the night before.

"Did you and your husband get along?"

"Wait! Is this about *me* now?" She exclaimed. "You ask me to come down here to assist with the investigation and you think I did it? Am I a suspect?"

"To be honest, ma'am, everyone in your husband's close circle is a suspect until we can cross them off the list."

Jackson was not one to beat around the bush.

"Of course, Mark and I got along," she answered. "Like all couples, we had our disagreements, but we always found a way to resolve them for the sake of our boys—who by the way, I must get back to now. They're taking the loss of their father really hard and it's not the nanny's job to be with them at a time like this."

"You're right, Mrs. Bridges. You should be there with your children. Thank you for coming by the station. If we learn anything or have any more questions, we'll be sure to contact you."

Camila stood up and flattened the front of her skirt with the brush of a hand. "Thank you."

Sam Jackson felt exhausted by the time Camila Bridges walked out of the door. He picked up his empty mug from the corner of his desk and dashed to the kitchen.

"You too?" Wendy Kenna asked him. She was standing at the counter sipping her second cup of cappuccino for the day.

"That Bridges woman's a piece of work. I should've let you tackle her instead." He poured himself a cup of coffee.

"No, thank you! As sad as it was having to break the news that her husband was killed, I could hardly believe the arrogance in the woman. At first, I thought it was her grief that made her seem so rude, but I quickly learned that's just her."

"You're talking about when she cursed out the nanny in front of us and ordered her to leave?"

"Yep. That's a part of it, but her demeanor threw me off after we broke the news," Kenna said. "Of course, there were the initial tears, but those wore off rather quickly, I'd say."

Jackson was nodding. "In the office just now too."

"But her alibi last night checked out," Kenna told him.

"It did, huh?"

"Yep. She couldn't have been two places at once. Unless…"

"She had someone do the deed," he replied. "But of course, this is all guesswork. The woman could be as clean as a whistle."

"You're right."

"Any leeway with the nurse?"

She nodded. "A number of displeased former patients. She gave me a list of names she could recall."

"Sounds like this guy and his wife might've been made for each other." Jackson sipped his coffee.

"By what I've been hearing so far, I can't agree more."

* * * *

"Have you heard the awful news, Father?" Sue McCloud asked Joe on the porch of the rectory.

"You're referring to the murdered doctor?"

"I guess you've heard."

She sat down next to him.

"It's been all over the radio and TV stations, and everyone's talking about it. I'm surprised you just reached with the news. You're usually my antenna."

She laughed. "You're calling me a gossip?"

"No…you're not that bad, Sue. But on a serious note, it's really sad what happened. A doctor getting gunned down in his office—the place he spent treating people who needed the help."

"You do realize that man was Melanie Robinson's doctor, don't you?"

He was clearly shocked. "I wasn't aware of that. Wow. What a surprise. I wonder if Todd…"

"Had anything to do with it?"

"I was going to say that I wonder if he heard the news," Joe quickly replied.

58

"I'm sure Agatha would've told him. She said she was headed to his house after work because she didn't wanna talk about it over the phone."

Joe shook his head. "Seems like it's always something. Isn't it?"

Sue slowly nodded.

"First, his wife dies and her doctor the day of her funeral."

"You do know how that sounds right?" Sue looked at him, curiously.

"Things happen, Sue. Sometimes, they appear to have a deeper meaning when they're purely coincidental. I don't know Todd all that well, but I'm sure he's got a steady head on his shoulders."

"But if we can see how the two coincided... I mean... Melanie's death, then her doctor's on the same day of her funeral, don't you think the police are looking at that same picture?" Sue pressed.

"What are you—a detective now, Sue? You're thinking too deeply. I'm sure that there are some bright minds on the police force."

"Well, I'm not too sure about that!" She folded her arms. "Are you forgetting what Old

Providence's best and brightest almost did to my Mike? If it wasn't for you doing the *real* detective work, he would've been incarcerated today."

Joe was quiet for a moment.

"The Lord was on Mike's side," he finally said. "And whoever killed that doctor— regardless of their reasoning, will be brought to justice. I'm confident of that."

"I'm not so confident," Sue replied.

"Oh? Why not?"

"Because the brightest minds around here aren't on the police force." She got up. "I have to go. Where's that boy of mine?"

"Probably helping Mister Pickling somewhere on the grounds."

"Shoots! Now, I have to go looking for him."

"He does have a cell phone, you know?" He tilted his eyeglasses.

"Oh! I forgot!"

"And look who's talking about the *brightest minds*!"

She giggled. "You're too much, Father."

* * * *

"Sorry about the wait, Miss Caddel," Detective Jackson told Heather.

"It's okay," she said.

"Please follow me to my office."

He led the way and as she took a seat in his office, he shut the door behind them.

"Let me start by offering my sincerest condolences for the loss of your employer," he said, sitting at the desk across from her.

"Thank you."

"The purpose of asking you to come here is so that we can gather as much information as possible to assist us in finding the person responsible for murdering Doctor Bridges."

"Yes, sir."

"How long have you been employed by the doctor?"

"Five months," Heather replied.

"How was everything going at the office?" he asked.

"Normal, I guess."

"Did you enjoy working there?"

"Sure. I have no complaints."

"Uh—huh. So, did everyone get along with Doctor Bridges?" he probed.

"You mean—all the staff members?"

"Yes."

"Yes—everyone got along with him just fine," she replied.

Jackson shifted in his seat a bit. "So, there was nothing out of the ordinary that happened at work?"

Heather shrugged. "I'm not sure I understand what you mean, Detective."

"What about the patients? Were any of them disgruntled or upset at Doctor Bridges during the time you were in his employ?"

"Sure, there were. At least four patients since I've been working there," she revealed. "Only a few weeks ago, a couple were there and the husband pretty much told Doctor Bridges off. He was upset about the level of care the doctor had given his wife."

"Do you remember the conversation?" Jackson asked.

"How could I forget?"

Heather went on to relay the whole story.

"He said something about Doctor Bridges reaping what he'd sown and paying for what he'd done to his wife. And that the doctor's children would pay too."

"His children?" Jackson grimaced.

"Yeah. That's what he said. I mean...I can understand why anyone would be upset in this man's position. I remember when his wife first came to our office, she was full of life, looked healthy and vibrant and after she'd sought Doctor Bridge's care, months later, she was barely recognizable. The husband claimed that Doctor Bridges had talked them into a procedure that wasn't necessary and it ruined his wife's life. I'm just telling you this because you asked if anything had happened at the office. I'm not saying that I believe this man had anything to do with Doctor Bridges' death. Let me just make that clear."

"What's the name of the couple?"

"Todd and Melanie Robinson. I'm sure you're already in possession of Mrs. Robinson's file along with all the other ones."

"Tell me more," Jackson said.

Heather went on to share incidences involving other irate patients and she spent the better part of an hour doing so. Jackson emptied his cup of coffee, mostly sipping it after it had already turned cold as he jotted down every bit of information he deemed might be useful.

"I'd say, based on what you just told me, that your workplace has seen quite a bit of drama as of late," he said.

"I'm afraid so." She grinned, nervously.

He studied her for a moment. "Tell me about yesterday—the last day your boss was seen alive. Describe that day for me."

Heather arched her brows while giving it some thought. "Well, it was a pretty typical day. Nurse June and I, along with Doctor Bridges were looking forward to a surprise farewell party we were throwing that afternoon for a co-worker who was leaving."

"What's the name of this co-worker?" Jackson asked.

"Cherry Granger."

"Do you know why she was leaving?"

"She was retiring early to go back to the Cayman Islands where she's from originally," she answered.

"So, she left on good terms?"

"Oh—yes! She was the longest serving employee at the office whom Doctor Bridges had relied on. Although he had a way about him that some people didn't really find *inviting*, for lack of a better word, Cherry always understood him and encouraged us—well *me* to not take things too personally. To kind of let it roll off my back, you know?"

"Things like what?"

"Well, for instance, sometimes he could address you in an abrupt manner or direct you to do something in front of patients that made you look inferior. At least, that's how he managed to make me feel sometimes," she explained.

"Did you resent Doctor Bridges for making you feel that way?" he probed.

"Resent? No. When I first started working there, I didn't like some of the things he said and did, and I was thinking of finding another job, but after Cherry talked to me and explained that he really was a nice person at heart—that he wasn't all bad, I stopped feeling badly when he was just, I guess—being himself."

"I understand," Jackson replied. "So, you mentioned a party…"

"Yes, we had it yesterday after work right at the office. We ate, danced and had a great time. Cherry was thrilled that we thought enough to celebrate her before she left," she replied.

"What time did the party end?"

"A little after six. It started right after four o'clock."

"Who was the first to leave?"

"Cherry did. She had a plane to catch that evening."

"I see."

"Nurse June and I left afterwards and Doctor Bridges said he was gonna work for another hour or so before going home," she said.

"Did he seem worried about anything, as far as you could tell?."

Heather thought for a moment. "No. Not at all. He was actually in a pretty good mood all day, which was hardly the case most days."

After jotting down the last bit of relevant information, Jackson put the pen down. "Okay. That's all for now, Miss Caddel. We'll reach out to you if there's anything more that we need. You've been a tremendous help."

"Thank you, Detective Jackson."

He got up and opened the door for her. "If there's anything else you can think of that you feel may be relevant to this investigation, please don't hesitate to give me a call." He handed her his card.

Glancing down at it, she replied, "Will do."

7

Can I get you another one?"
Julio Domingo asked Cherry as
she sat alone at the counter.

She glanced at her empty beer can and
the glass next to it. "That would be great.
Thanks, Julio."

Julio was in his late sixties but had been
blessed with a youthful face and an amazing
physique. He had a shoulder-length ponytail and
the whitest beard Cherry had seen on a man.
Although he managed the place, he also served
drinks at the bar during the day.

"One beer coming up!" he said while a
middle-aged black man walked inside and
proceeded over to the bar.

Julio handed Cherry the beer and
retrieved the empty can from nearby.

"Thank you," she said.

He then diverted his attention towards the
stranger. "What are you having, sir?"

The man looked at Cherry. "Whatever she's having."

Cherry glanced at the guy who stood at approximately six feet tall, had tight short curly hair and a dimple on his chin. By the way he was staring, she figured he found her attractive, but she was not in the mood to care.

"One beer coming right up!" Julio said, happily.

"Do you mind?" The man was now standing next to her.

"Feel free." Cherry took a gulp of her beer.

He sat down and Julio placed the beer in front of him, then made himself busy on the other side of the counter where a few men were seated.

"My name's James. May I ask yours?" The man asked Cherry in a gentle voice.

"I'm really not in the mood," she answered. "If you're here to pick somebody up, it's not gonna be me."

"I'm sorry; I didn't mean to disturb you. I'll just shut up." He picked up his beer.

Feeling a tinge of guilt, Cherry looked at him. "Please, don't mind me. I'm just not having such a great day; it's not your fault."

"I'm sorry to hear that. Is there anything I can do?"

She sighed. "I'm afraid not. My name's Cherry, by the way. Cherry Granger." She extended her hand.

"Nice to meet you, Cherry. My last name's Edmon.

"Nice to meet you James Edmon." She laughed.

"Ahh...that's it! You laughed."

"I guess I did!"

Julio glanced over at them a few times as he shined some wine glasses.

Minutes later, a group of college kids entered the pub and were chatting quite loudly amongst themselves. Eventually, Cherry and James took their conversation to one of the empty tables in a corner of the room.

"You come here a lot?" James asked her. He was almost halfway through his beer.

"Nope...but I will be," she replied. "I happen to own the place."

"Really?"

"Yep. I inherited it from my uncle. Julio there, the bartender, runs it for me."

"Wow. That's...that's great! I wish I had an uncle who'd leave me a bar."

Cherry laughed.

"Well, I can see you're in a better mood now."

She nodded slowly and smiled. "Maybe it's the company."

"I'm flattered."

"I owe you an apology."

"For what?" he asked.

"For the attitude I gave you after you came over. It's just that a few days ago, I was told that my former boss, a surgeon, had been murdered in his office," she revealed.

"I'm so sorry to hear that. Where did this happen?"

"Not here on the island. It was in Old Providence where I'd spent the last two decades of my life. I just moved back here. And to get the news that he'd been killed is a lot to digest."

"That's terrible, Cherry. Seems like you and your boss had a good relationship."

"We did. Honestly, he could be a pain in the butt at times, but he was okay. Kept me employed for nineteen years."

"Sounds like an overall okay guy."

"I guess you could say that," she agreed. "But enough about me. So, what do you do?"

"I'm a pilot. I actually own a charter company near the airport, a couple of planes."

"Wow! And you talk about wishing you had an uncle who'd leave you a bar! You're a mess, James!"

"Was just pulling your leg." He laughed. "But I am impressed by what you have here, the fact that you're a young entrepreneur, and even as you said, recently retired from the nine to five rat race. That's admirable. You're a well-accomplished lady."

"And given your achievements, being fairly young yourself, I don't have the words to describe you."

"Fairly young, huh?" He smiled.

Cherry chuckled.

The two spoke for a while as James was intent on getting to know her much better.

* * * *

"Bring in those cases of wine for me when you get a chance," Joe told Stewart Pickling. "And remember, I have a mental count of how much are out there, so don't let the devil fool you today."

"Yes, Father." Pickling laughed as he headed out to Joe's car.

Joe was at the rectory getting ready for a counseling session he was having in a few minutes with the Daltons—a young couple who were already facing infidelity in their marriage.

Fifty-nine-year-old Stewart Pickling was a caretaker of the church grounds and a handyman. Joe often called him a jack of all trades. However, Pickling had the tendency to get a little tipsy whenever he got his hands on a bottle of wine he either snuck from the church or purchased at the bar just around the corner from where he lived. He was usually smart enough not to show up at work drunk and the couple of times he wasn't, Joe reprimanded him and sent him home.

"Is that the last one?" Joe asked, as he hurried from a back room.

Pickling had assembled the cases against a wall near the front door.

"Yes, sir. That's all of it."

Joe went over and had a look to ensure that a bottle or two weren't missing.

"Okay, thanks, old pal." He patted Pickling on the shoulder.

"No worries, Father. I'll be out back if you need anything else."

Pickling went outside and sat down on a stoop directly beneath the crape myrtle tree. He opened the brown paper bag he'd brought from home and unwrapped the triple decker egg salad sandwich he'd prepared early that morning.

A stray dog that wandered around the church grounds soon made its way over to him.

"You hungry, mutt?" he asked the dog after taking a bite into his sandwich.

The look in the dog's eyes spoke volumes.

"Okay." He pinched off a piece of his sandwich and tossed it in the animal's direction. "Here ya go!"

The dog quickly ate it up, then looked to Pickling for more.

"Look—I'm hungry too, ya know! And a much harder worker than you are!" He pinched off another piece of his sandwich and tossed it. "Now, take that and go."

Again, the dog ate and immediately, looked to Pickling for more.

"No! No more! Go on your way now!"

It didn't move—only gave him another pitiful look.

"Shucks! Here—take it all!" He threw down what was left of his sandwich. "And after you eat that up, get the hell outta here!"

Pickling got up and walked off angrily. He might not have had much patience, but he couldn't be accused of not having a heart.

8

𝒯he body of Dr. Mark Bridges was released to his family for burial ten days after the shooting.

The funeral was held at the local Presbyterian church that he and his family faithfully attended.

At the graveyard, Detectives Wendy Kenna and Sam Jackson stood a short distance away from the crowd and quietly observed. Camila Bridges and her sons sat under the tent with relatives and members of Bridges' staff who'd come to pay their last respects. Beulah had shown up and was sitting next to Cherry Granger who'd flown in on her new friend James' charter flight. Father Joe McCullen, who also felt the need to be there even though he didn't know the family, stood near the tent. Glancing behind, he spotted the detectives right away.

Camila and her sons Mark Jr., fourteen and William, twelve were drenched with tears.

Camila was hollering while her boys quietly wept.

"Here we go again…" Jackson muttered.

Kenna quickly wiped the smile off her face. "That woman is too much!"

Cherry was overwhelmed with sadness as she viewed the casket hovering just above the ground and Beulah held her hand.

At the end of the service, after he'd offered his condolences to Camila and her children, Joe walked over to the detectives to say hello.

"Good afternoon, Father," Jackson said.

"Hi, Father," Kenna added.

"I don't need to ask what brings you two here."

Jackson smiled. "I guess you don't, Father."

Just then, Todd Robinson, dressed in a pair of black jeans and a black shirt, passed them by and was walking in the direction of the tent.

"Todd!" Joe called out to him.

But Todd continued on, only stopping in front of the gravesite where the casket bearing the body of Dr. Mark Bridges was slowly being lowered. He stood there for a moment, then leaned over and spat on the casket.

"See…I told you you'd pay for what you did to my wife." He scoffed. "I hope you burn in hell!"

Those who were witnesses to the disturbing scene gasped.

Joe and the detectives were already running toward him when Mark Jr. dashed over to attack the man who had the gall to blatantly desecrate his father's grave. And other men on the scene rushed to intervene.

"You bastard!" the boy shouted before delivering a high-powered blow to Todd's mid-section.

Todd stumbled, nearly falling inside the open grave, but someone caught him just in time. By then, Jackson had grabbed hold of the boy who was screaming expletives and Kenna was doing her best to barricade the scene. Camila Bridges was demanding that Jackson take his grimy hands off her son while Joe was helping to keep Todd back. He caught a whiff of the alcohol on his breath and knew it was the culprit behind the most disgraceful act.

"Okay, that's enough!" Kenna exclaimed.

Jackson released his grip on Mark after he'd managed to calm him down. Immediately, Todd Robinson was placed under arrest and was escorted to the detectives' black SUV.

"I'm very sorry," Joe apologized emphatically to the family. The boys were now again in tears, but for a very different reason. "That should never have happened."

"You're damn right!" Camila replied. "I'm gonna see to it that whoever that brute of a human being is pays dearly for how he's traumatized my boys." She glared at Kenna. "You officers had better look long and hard at that man in your vehicle. Without a shred of doubt in my heart, he's the one that murdered my husband!"

She grabbed her children by the arms and marched toward the parking lot.

* * * *

"What a scene that was!" Sue exclaimed when she heard the news the next day. She was in the kitchen putting a lunch platter she'd brought for the priest in the refrigerator.

Sitting in his recliner, Joe sighed. "In all my years, I've never seen anything like that, Sue.

What could've possibly possessed Todd to go down there to the man's funeral and spit on his grave?"

"The alcohol got the best of him," she replied.

"Surely, but even so…" He sighed again. "I guess the pain of losing Melanie was so great, he became vulnerable to the devil's vices. He made himself look guilty as sin now."

"Yep. He dug that nail into the coffin for sure." Sue walked into the living room and sat down. "I'd say out of many, he's the number one suspect."

Joe nodded, then sat up straight. "As guilty as he looks though, I'm not convinced that he killed anyone."

Sue looked at him as if he was terribly confused. "You're not?"

"No. I'm not. It doesn't make sense— none of it does. If Todd murdered the doctor, why would he make such a scene at the funeral? To me, he wanted to get back at the doctor in any way he could while the body was still above ground. If he was the one who murdered him, in my opinion, he wouldn't have been compelled, under the influence of alcohol or not, to do what he did yesterday."

Sue considered his point. "You might be making sense, Father. Although I'm not completely convinced."

"I know I am."

"He's still locked up?" she asked.

"I heard he's being released on bail sometime today."

"If your assumption is right, I wish him all the luck in the world."

Just then, the phone rang and Sue got up to answer it.

"The rectory," she said.

A moment later, she brought the handset over to Joe. "It's for you. Wally Profado."

She now had a frown on her face as the very sound of Wally's voice and utterance of his name, even from her own tongue, left a bad taste in her mouth.

"Yes, Wally. How are ya?" Joe said.

Sue soon noticed a change in his expression.

"Uh—huh… Uh—huh," he said. "Okay. Thanks so much for calling."

Joe looked at Sue. "Wally just told me that Todd Robinson has been named their prime suspect and they're building a case against him."

"So, he's not gonna be released on bail anymore?" she asked.

"Yes, he'll be released, but they plan to re-arrest him first chance they get. Wally wanted me to know that he's not on the case, so he has no influence in the investigation. He encouraged me to try and get Todd to confess to the crime so that this whole thing wouldn't get really ugly really fast. Apparently, Mrs. Bridges knows some people in high places who can easily put Todd away for life if he doesn't come clean and strike some sort of a deal beforehand. I must do something." He got up and sauntered over to the window. "But it's not what Wally suggested."

"What are you gonna do, Father?" Sue probed.

"Other than pay Todd a visit when he gets out…I have no idea. Time will tell."

2

_____

*A*fter Todd was released on bail, he met Joe McCullen sitting on his front porch reading the newspaper.

"Todd! You're back!" Joe stood up as he mounted the steps.

"What are you doing here, Father?" Todd asked while he inserted his key into the doorknob.

"I'm here to have a word with you." Joe tucked the newspaper under his arm.

"I don't wanna talk about it. I know I did a dumb thing." He pushed the door open and headed into the house.

"Do you mind if I come in? I won't take up too much of your time."

Todd looked back at him and shrugged. "Whatever."

Joe was standing in the middle of the living room as Todd headed to the kitchen for a drink of water.

"You want something to drink, Father? I'm afraid that water is all I have for now."

"No, thanks. I'm fine."

Todd walked back over with his water.

"You might as well sit down," he said. "I'm going to."

"Yes, right!" Joe took the sofa.

He couldn't help noticing that Todd looked a wreck. He was unshaven and his hair was disheveled.

"How did they treat you in there?" Joe asked him.

"Decent, considering the circumstances."

Joe leaned forward in his seat. "Before Melanie passed, I promised her right in front of you that I will look out for you. Remember that?"

Todd nodded. "I remember, but I don't need you to do that, Father. I'm a grown man."

"You are. But as grown as many of us are, we all still need one another. To this day, I need the good people in my life to keep me grounded and on the right track. I'm a priest, but I'm not perfect. I have my moments when I must think twice because some silly thought came to mind or I was about to make some stupid decision. Without people looking out for me, I don't know what state I'd be in today."

Todd seemed somehow enlightened by Joe's words.

"And that's the same for everyone," Joe added. "That's the way we were intended to be—a community of people who look out for one another and offer a helping hand when one of us falls down. I'm here to give you that helping hand."

Todd took a drink of his water, then rested the glass on the side table.

He looked at the priest. "So, you're not gonna ask me?"

"Ask you what?"

"If I killed that guy?"

"Nope."

"You don't wanna know if I did it?"

"Only if you want to share that information with me." Joe interlaced his fingers.

Todd looked confused. "You mean...you're not curious?" he asked.

Joe shook his head. "Not really."

Todd was becoming slightly agitated. "Why not? Are all you pastors that naïve? Or is it that you think I'm innocent only because you're forcing yourself to dismiss the other possibility?"

Joe looked intently into his eyes. "The reason why I'm not wondering about your guilt or innocence is because even though I don't know you all that well, Todd, I did know Melanie enough to be convinced that she would've never married a man capable of killing another human being for the sake of revenge. You and I both know what she stood for. I'm aware that despite your absence from church for the most part, you are a man of faith, you know right from wrong and you are clearly aware that there are consequences to your actions, including what you did yesterday."

Todd shook his head. "You're right, Father—about everything. I didn't kill that bastard, but I'm surely glad someone did! I know the way I feel about that is wrong, but it's just the way I feel. Sometimes I wish I'd been man enough to pull the trigger myself, but like you said, I knew it would've been wrong and Mel never would've approved. Knowing how she looked at things and looked at me is what stopped me from retaliating in other ways.

But…I guess the decision I made to have a few drinks yesterday clouded my judgment."

"I understand that," Joe replied. "But now, your clouded judgment has made you a prime suspect in the investigation surrounding the doctor's death."

"Why am I not surprised?"

"I'm not either. You pretty much made their job easy for them. Although the man reportedly had a lot of enemies, you've been understandably singled out. Lord knows if they'll even bother to get in touch with the others on the list of suspects."

Todd was nodding. "I guess this is a consequence of my actions like you just talked about."

"Yep. But we all do stupid things sometimes. The first thing I would suggest is you reach out to the man's family with an apology, letting them know you weren't in your right frame of mind when you entered that graveyard. The second thing you should do is retain the services of a good attorney. There's a guy who attends our church who's a fabulous lawyer. I can give you his name…"

"I don't need any lawyer, Father," Todd replied. "And I'm surely not apologizing to that butcher's family for anything."

"But you said yourself you knew you shouldn't have done it," Joe said.

"I did. But I never said I was sorry. The truth is—I'm not. And I'm not apologizing."

Joe was almost at a loss for words. He was becoming convinced that Todd still wasn't thinking clearly.

"Look—that can come in time," he rebutted. "But at least get an attorney to stand with you through this."

"Nope." He was adamant in his stance. "No lawyers."

"Is there anything I can do to change your mind, Todd?"

"Nothing—although I do appreciate your concern, Father."

Just then, they heard a car pull up in front of the yard and moments later, steps hurrying toward the front door. Todd stood up.

"Todd!"

They both recognized the voice.

"It's me—Agatha!"

He opened the door and she walked inside.

"I knew I recognized your car, Father," she said.

"Yep. That's old faithful," Joe replied.

She then focused her attention on Todd. "What on earth have you done, Todd? How could you do something like that?"

"Agatha, I don't need this. Like I told Father Joe here—I know it was a dumb thing to do."

"But why did you do that? Everyone's talking about it!"

"I was drunk, okay? I was frigging drunk!"

He sat down.

"Todd, you've got to get a hold of yourself." Agatha slid her purse off her shoulder. "You're carrying on like a runaway train!"

"Don't you think I know that?" he snarled.

Joe sighed. "I've been trying to get him to retain the services of an attorney since now it's highly probable that they're building a case against him for murder," Joe told her.

"But Todd's no murderer. He's done a stupid thing at the funeral, but I can assure you he's incapable of killing another person."

"I don't need you to vouch for me, Agatha," Todd said. "You two keep going on about my not being capable of murder, but the truth is—I *am* guilty! I had a hand in that beast murdering my wife because I took her there week after week for months! Even when I saw that she wasn't getting any better." Tears rolled down his face. "I waited too late to try and seek out other specialists. By then, there was nothing anyone could do. So, you two can go on and on about how I'm no murderer, but the fact is: I am! And I deserve to pay dearly for it!"

He got up and stormed into the master bedroom, slamming the door behind him.

"I see what's happening here." Agatha stood up and began pacing the floor.

"Yep. He wants to be punished for the fact that Melanie died and he couldn't protect her," Joe said.

"But he's got it all wrong, Father!" Agatha stopped in her tracks. "That man did everything he possibly could to help Mel through that ordeal. I've watched him reach out to doctors pleading with them to help her, but there was nothing they could do. There was nothing anyone could do after Doctor Bridges performed that botched procedure on her."

She shook her head and found a chair. "We can't let him destroy himself, Father. He doesn't care if they pin the murder on him because he feels he deserves it and has nothing to live for." Agatha was clearly heartbroken.

Joe knew that she was right. Todd Robinson was in deep despair and he feared for his wellbeing. He got up and went to the bedroom door, lightly pressing his ear against it.

"Todd…"

"Go away, Father!" he answered tearfully.

"I'd like to pray with you if you don't mind."

"I do mind. I just need you guys to leave me be; give me my space!"

"Okay, we'll do that, Todd. But promise me that you'll call me anytime—day or night whenever you're ready to talk."

There was silence.

"Todd…"

"Yeah. I hear you. Just, please go."

Respecting his wishes, Joe and Agatha left the house, ensuring that the door was locked behind them.

"I'm afraid for him," Agatha stated, sadly as they walked toward their cars. "There's no telling what he'll do next. I've never, ever seen him like this!"

Joe took her hand. "We must pray for him, Agatha. That's the best thing we can do since we can't control any person or their actions. We must keep him covered."

"Yes, Father."

"In the meantime, I need to try and find out some more about this Doctor Bridges."

"Have you spoken to Beulah?"

"Beulah, who?"

"Hart. She was at the funeral—told me when I ran into her at the food store this morning. She used to work for him, you know."

Joe arched a brow. "I wasn't aware of that. And I wasn't aware that she was at the funeral," he replied.

"Yes, she was there, but she'd left before the commotion started. I can have her call you if you'd like."

"That would be wonderful."

Joe saw Agatha off, then drove away himself after saying a short prayer in his car for Todd and sealing it with the sign of the cross.

10

*T*wo days later…

Beulah Hart was wearing a white pants suit and dark shades when she walked into the coffee shop. Reading the top story in the newspaper, Joe had no idea she'd arrived until she sat down at the table.

"Hi, Father Joe," she said, folding her shades and resting them on the table.

"Beulah!" His eyes lit up when he saw her. "How are you?"

"I'm well. How have you been?"

"Great! My goodness! It's been such a long time. Seems almost like a lifetime ago."

"Yes, it was," she replied. "At least twenty years."

"Agatha told me you were at the doctor's funeral the other day," he said.

"I was. She told me you were too. There was such a good turnout, so no wonder we didn't see each other."

"Good thing the graveyard service wasn't too long because these knees of mine sometimes act up."

She smiled.

"Ready to come back to the church?" He was hopeful.

"Father, you know that can't happen."

"There's no such thing as can't, dear."

Beulah Hart had left the church when she was thirteen years old. Her parents had decided that they no longer believed its teachings and had declared themselves agnostics. After they left, they never looked back.

"I must admit when Agatha told me you wanted me to call, I wasn't sure how I felt about it because she didn't say why," Beulah said.

"I'm glad you did."

"When you told me what was happening, I knew I had to help any way that I could."

"You're still that wonderful person you've always been, Beulah, and I'm glad to see that."

She reached over to the chair next to her and retrieved a mini notebook from her bag. Opening it up, she tore off the first page and slid it over to Joe.

"It's all there," she said. "The ones she thought stood out the most."

Joe perused the handwritten list of names and addresses. There were ten in total.

"This is great," he replied. "It should be a great help."

"Oh! And the name of the brother is at the top of the list," she said. "My friend thinks you should start there—and I must agree. He called the office several times even while I was working there and the two of them had some really volatile conversations. Ted's address wasn't kept on file, but my friend was once sent to deliver a package to his place of business and she remembered the address.

"Perfect! Thanks for letting me know."

"It's a good thing she kept her old computer and had backed up the data. There was no other way to access any of the files since they're currently in police custody."

"She's a smart girl. Please thank her for me."

Beulah slid out her cell phone and clicked the speed dial. "You can thank her yourself."

She handed the phone to him.

"Cherry?" he said after a woman had picked up. "It's Father Joe McCullen. Beulah is sitting here with me."

"Oh! Hi, Father Joe! It's nice to meet you although at quite a distance," she replied, energetically.

Cherry Granger was sitting at her computer desk while James was stretched off on the couch behind her, fast asleep. The two had become very close and Cherry was convinced that he was the one for her.

"I want to thank you for going out on a limb to provide this information for me," Joe told her. "And rest assured, this stays between the three of us."

"Whatever I can do to help, Father. Beulah has spoken very highly of you—said she trusts you with her life. For her to have that much confidence in a person, says a lot."

"Well, that's news to me, but good to hear." Joe grinned. "How's Grand Cayman, by the way?"

Smiling, she turned and glanced at James. "It's fabulous. Just fabulous."

"That's wonderful. Feel like I've known you forever even though we've only just met."

"The feeling is mutual, Father."

"Well, good speaking with you. I'll turn the phone over to your friend. Take care."

"You too, Father Joe!"

He handed the phone to Beulah who spoke with Cherry for a few moments.

After ending the call, she slipped the phone back into her purse and looked at Joe. "So, I guess that's it then?"

"Yes. Thanks so much, Beulah," Joe replied. "I really appreciate everything both of you are doing to help bring justice to the late Doctor Bridges and to clear the name of a good man."

"You're very welcome, Father. I hope it helps."

She started to get up.

"Wait! Aren't you staying for coffee?"

"Oh, I wouldn't mind at all. Was so caught up in the purpose of the meeting, I forgot this is a coffee shop!"

"No worries. It's self-service here, so I'll have to go to the counter and place the order. What will you be having?"

"French vanilla if they have it," she said.

"French vanilla and a cappuccino it is!"
He got up and headed for the counter.

* * * *

Two hours later...

"Hey there, Mister Bridges! How are you doing today?" Joe said as he walked toward the man tending to a speedboat.

Joe had made the drive to Providence Bay – an area of Old Providence where a number of marine companies and shipyards were located.

"Okay," the man replied, not allowing Joe to interrupt the flow of his work.

"The young lady inside the building there told me I could find you around back," Joe indicated as he finally approached. "I'm Father Joe McCullen. I was wondering if I can have a word with you, if you don't mind."

Ted was the only person Joe had seen when he rounded the bend to the open area behind the building. More than a dozen boats of various sizes were scattered about the yard. Some in what appeared to be pristine condition and others in a clear state of disrepair.

Ted, a man in his sixties, was wiping off one of the newer models with a white rag. He soon stopped what he was doing and tossed the rag on the rim of a bucket nearby.

"What can I do for you, Father? As you can see, I'm busy here."

"Yes, I can see that," Joe replied. "I was wondering if I can speak with you about your brother Mark."

"What about him?" Ted looked at him suspiciously.

"Well, a dear lady from my parish used to be in his care…"

"What? He took her money and screwed her over like the numerous stories I've heard over the years?"

"Unfortunately, she passed away," Joe informed him.

"I'm sorry to hear that. Maybe she should've found a better doctor. Look—my brother had a specialty and wasn't curing or even trying to find cures for his patients. His specialty and only concern was making money—getting his hands on it the best way he could. But with that said, what does your parishioner dying have to do with me?"

Joe knew he had to think quickly if he was going to keep Ted talking.

"Her husband, whom I know is innocent, may be implicated in your brother's murder and I'm trying to get to the bottom of it."

"That wouldn't be the guy who spat on Mark's grave. Would it?"

Reluctantly, Joe nodded.

"Kudos to that guy! He had real guts!" Ted said happily, much to Joe's surprise. "If he didn't kill the bastard, I know the real killer's surely glad that someone else is in the limelight. But if you came here wondering if I might've offed my brother, I'm gonna tell you the same thing I told the cops which is I had no use for Mark same way he had no use for me after he stole the forty grand I gave him to invest on my behalf. Many times since then, I wanted to strangle him and the only thing stopping me were those two boys who actually loved their dad. Trust me, if it wasn't for them, I would've done the deed myself." He picked up his rag again. "Now, good day, Father. I've got work to do. Good luck."

"Thank you for your time, Mister Bridges." Joe nodded before walking away.

"Father!" Ted called out to him moments later.

Joe stopped and turned around.

"The killer may have been closer to my brother than you think. You might want to start with that gold-digging wife of his Camila. She's had more reasons to want Mark dead than all his enemies combined."

* * * *

That night...

"Camila Bridges was checked out thoroughly, Father." Wally said to Joe over the phone. "Her husband allegedly had numerous affairs over the course of their marriage and apparently, she threatened to divorce him and leave him penniless on countless occasions. But despite that, they stayed together and by all accounts—family and friends—they've been getting along better than ever within the past few years."

"I see." Joe adjusted his eyeglasses and peered at the list of names Beulah had handed to him.

"Father, as I told you before, if you want to help Todd Robinson, you need to get him to confess and he will stand a better chance. After all, he's grieving the loss of his wife whom he feels is dead at the hands of her doctor. The courts will show lenience."

"Why should I convince a man to confess to a crime he isn't guilty of, Wally?"

"You really believe that, Father? Even after the commotion he caused at the man's burial?"

"Yes, I do," Joe replied.

Wally sighed heavily.

"What do you know about Fiona Wright?"

"Fiona Wright? You mean—one of Doctor Bridges' former patients?" Wally asked.

"Uh—huh. And Ian Miller."

"Wait. Where are you getting these names from?"

"That's not important, Wally. Let's stay focused here."

"Father, you need to leave the investigation to the police."

"What investigation? Do you know if an investigation is taking place?" Joe replied, sarcastically.

"Okay…so, we're playing that game?" Wally shook his head. "All I can tell you is that Mrs. Wright's guardian Brian Bakshi and Mister Miller have both been questioned by police and they're not suspects. That's all I'm saying."

"Thank you, Wally. Have a good night's sleep." Joe said. And he hung up the phone.

After switching off the lamp nearby, he stretched out in bed, placed his hands behind his head and gazed up at the ceiling. Revisiting the conversation he had with Ted Bridges, he recalled the statement he'd made about Mark's killer being *close* to him. If the perpetrator wasn't his own wife, then who could it possibly be?

Undoubtedly, Joe knew he had a task ahead of him. Todd Robinson's life was on the line—a man who couldn't care less how it all turned out.

11

*T*hree weeks later...

Sisters Angelica and Gertrude were playing volleyball on the church grounds with a group of teenage girls. The girls all attended a boarding school supported by the local diocese. Some of their schoolmates observing from the bleachers were giggling and quietly telling jokes about the nuns running around in their habits.

Joe watched from the bottom row of the bleachers, making it clear to all which team he was rooting for.

"Go back! Go back!" he yelled at Mercedes, the server, whose foot was a few inches outside of the white line.

"Keep your mouth shut, Father Joe!" Gertrude, who was on the opposing team, barked.

Wiping the pebbles of sweat from her face, Angelica laughed. "Take your losses like a woman. There's no turning back now, Sister!"

Angelica knew she was getting underneath Gertrude's skin and was enjoying every minute of it. Gertrude cut her eye in retaliation and readied herself for when the ball came over.

In the piping hot sun, Joe was attempting to keep himself dry with a small white towel tossed across his shoulder. He didn't mind if he *cooked* in the sun, as he often said, since he loved the games the church hosted every other weekend.

"Wake up!" Gertrude told Doria, the blonde slightly crouched at her right. "You look like you're about to topple over!"

Angelica shook her head. Gertrude was clearly too competitive for her own good.

Mercedes hit the volleyball over the net and Gertrude, Doria and another girl nearby all aimed to send it flying back.

"I've got it!" Mercedes yelled, just before Gertrude hit it directly into the net ahead.

"Bummer!" Gertrude muttered.

"Our game!" Angelica jumped up, excitedly. She and her teammates hugged and gave each other high fives.

As Gertrude walked off the court with her teammates, she said, "You've all done a good job, girls. Next time, we'll make their heads spin!" She gave them each a high five.

Joe smiled and went to meet them.

"Great job, everyone!" he said.

"Week after next, it'll be the boys' game and I'll show you all how it's done out here. For now, refreshments for everyone are over there at the table."

When he turned around, he saw Agatha Hall running toward the bleachers.

"Father, I need to speak with you," she said when she finally arrived.

They both stepped away from the others.

"What is it, Agatha?" he asked, concerned.

"I just got word that they've arrested Todd!"

Joe's heart sank. "I knew this was coming—just not this soon. Get Jim Cruz on the phone. Todd needs a good attorney, whether he wants one or not."

* * * *

Wendy Kenna was seated across the table from Todd Robinson while Sam Jackson quietly observed from the other side of the one-way glass. Todd's hands were cuffed and his feet shackled.

"For the record, Mister Robinson…are you stating that you're not interested in having an attorney present?" Kenna asked him.

"That's exactly what I'm saying, Detective," Todd replied, coolly.

"After you were arrested this morning, you expressed that you wanted to come clean regarding what you know about the murder of Doctor Mark Bridges. Am I correct?"

"Yes."

Kenna was taken aback by Todd's appearance when she saw him that day. He vaguely resembled the man she'd seen at the doctor's gravesite weeks earlier. Todd had lost a considerable amount of weight in that short time span and it was clear to her that he had not been taking care of himself. *'Maybe it's a combination of guilt and grief'*, she thought.

"I will ask you directly, Mister Robinson. Are you responsible for the death of Doctor Mark Bridges?" she asked.

"I am," he replied.

She looked intently into his eyes. "Did you discharge the weapon that killed Doctor Mark Bridges on June 29th, 2018?"

"I did."

"What type of weapon did you use?

"A 357 magnum," he answered without a blink.

"And where is that weapon now?" she asked.

"At the bottom of the Killarney River. I tossed it in there the night of the murder."

"This is too easy," Jackson muttered behind the glass. "It's too easy."

"What was your motive for murdering Doctor Bridges?"

Todd hesitated momentarily, then answered, "He killed my wife."

There was a brief pause in the room as Kenna was inwardly confronted by the gravity of those words.

She shifted to a more comfortable position in her chair. "Please explain the events leading up to the night of June 29th," she said.

"In late November of last year, my wife Melanie and I went to Doctor Bridges' office after we were referred there by another physician. Melanie had recently felt a strange growth in her mouth that wasn't there before, so she wanted to check it out. That day, Doctor Bridges took a sample for a biopsy and sent Mel home without any medications or antibiotics. Within an hour or two, she was in excruciating pain and called the office back to let the doctor know. But he wouldn't take the call; they said he was with a patient. Within twenty minutes or so, he returned the call and said she could take any over the counter pain killer and the use of antibiotics wasn't necessary. In the week we waited to get the results of the biopsy back, Mel was having a lot of headaches and pain around the area that was cut. I called back to the office a few times letting them know what was happening and Doctor Bridges assured me, through his staff, that the headaches would go away soon and said she should continue taking the pain medication. So, my wife did as was advised."

"Was she having any pain in the mouth or headaches before going to Doctor Bridges?" Kenna asked.

"None whatsoever. The growth was not painful for her at all. She was just concerned about what it was. And as for headaches—in all the years we've been married, Mel rarely ever got a headache and certainly none as excruciating as the ones she suffered after the procedure," he explained.

"Please continue."

"A week after the initial visit, we were called in for an appointment with Doctor Bridges. We were told that the results were in."

Todd seemed more uncomfortable at this point. He looked up at the ceiling, sighed deeply, and said, "Doctor Bridges broke the news that my wife had cancer."

Kenna felt his pain at that particular moment.

"But he said it was in its early stages and a surgery to remove all traces of the growth would be the solution. I asked if he was sure that Mel would be fine and he said that he was."

Todd looked into Kenna's eyes. "I would've done anything to save my wife, Detective— anything in this world. But something was telling me that if Mel really needed surgery, this guy shouldn't be the one to do it."

"Why did you feel that way?" she asked, curiously.

"I based it on the time he cut her for the sample and how careless he was with her. Sending her home without meds in the first place, etcetera. There was something about him I didn't like. I thought he was pompous and arrogant, and I told Mel what I thought about him. But despite all that, she wanted to let him do the surgery; said an acquaintance of hers highly recommended him." He shrugged. "It was her call."

"What was the cost of the surgery?"

"Fourteen thousand dollars. He said he was giving us a discount," Todd replied.

"Then what happened?"

He sighed again. "Well, before she went in for the surgery, I asked the doctor a second time if this procedure was going to heal my wife and he said she would be back to normal in no time. The headaches would go away and the other pain too. So, he performed the surgery. Mel found the recovery stage really difficult but was confident that once she healed up from it everything would be all right. But it didn't turn out that way."

"What happened?"

"About ten days later, Doctor Bridges put some sort of plate in her mouth to cover the opening where the growth used to be, but after he put it in, it fell out twice and he accused Mel of tampering with it with her tongue. But she swore she wasn't. I almost cursed him out for speaking to my wife like that, but Mel gestured for me to calm down and leave it alone. Boy! That was hard. By this time, Mel couldn't speak. Doctor Bridges said it would take a while since her tongue was quite heavy after the procedure. Well, after the plate dropped out a couple of times, he decided to leave it for a while."

"The plate that was supposed to cover the opening?" Kenna said.

"Yeah." He nodded. "That was another thing I didn't feel so good about. Three weeks passed and Mel still couldn't speak. She tried to form her words, but couldn't. And on top of that the headaches didn't stop. She was still having a great deal of pain. I asked the doctor why that was and he claimed Mel's body was taking longer than usual to heal and that we'd just have to be patient. Then one day, Mel indicated to me that she felt another growth in her mouth."

Kenna listened intently, almost in disbelief.

"Doctor Bridges said that another tumor had formed and he would need to go back in," Todd continued. "At that point, I'd had enough and I begged Mel to let me take her to another specialist, but still having faith in Bridges, she refused. So, we signed her up for another surgery that was supposed to take place eight days later."

"How much did this one cost?"

"Ten thousand. It's a good thing we had a decent savings, but those two procedures pretty much dried us up," Todd said. "But I didn't care about the money since I could always go out there and make more. I only wanted Mel to be well again."

He paused for a few moments. "After the second surgery, Mel started to deteriorate and all Doctor Bridges could say was that the cancer had spread and Mel wouldn't make it. I asked him how could that be when he promised that she would be fine. He claimed he wasn't God and wasn't in charge of a person's destiny."

"He said that?" Kenna grimaced and so did Jackson, still closely observing.

"He did," Todd replied. "That's when I took the decision-making out of Mel's hand and took her to another specialist. And then another and another. They all were horrified at the job Doctor Bridges had done in Mel's mouth and didn't want to touch his handiwork. I presume it had to do with potential lawsuits, not wanting to be implicated in any way if they were to get involved."

Kenna was nodding.

"Even though for the most part, they were tight-lipped, one surgeon said that Mel's condition shouldn't have deteriorated since, based on her initial diagnosis, it was completely curable. But Doctor Bridges had initially cut too deeply into the flesh while taking the sample for the biopsy, then by not ensuring that the plate was firmly in place after the first surgery, it caused the cancer to spread to other parts of her body. She was also supposed to do a brief round of chemo that never got off the ground."

"Why not?"

"Bridges never ordered it—I guess after he gave up on her. And we didn't know he did until it was too late." Todd said. "A few months later, Mel passed away. She'd never spoken a word after Bridges performed the first surgery. I never heard her voice again, her laugh. She used to sing in the kitchen while cooking and I never saw that again. And I never will."

Kenna wanted to tell him how sorry she was.

"So, eventually you and your wife paid Doctor Bridges a final visit obviously before her death?" she asked.

"Yes."

"How did that go?"

"Mel didn't want to go, but I convinced her that he needed to face us one last time for what he did to her," Todd replied. "I admit I was angry and hated him with a passion for how he treated my wife and I told him how I felt about him."

"You threatened him?"

"I told him I was a man of faith and that he would reap what he'd sown; that he'd pay for what he'd done and so would his children."

"What was his response to that?"

116

"Nothing."

"Nothing?"

"Right. Not to that. He only responded prior to that—making excuses for not giving Mel the proper care; claiming we knew what we were getting into—which was a bloody lie!"

"And the night of the murder? Tell me what happened," Kenna said.

"I was driving around that night trying to clear my head. It was the day my wife was buried."

"Uh—huh."

"I kept thinking about everything that happened and how walking into Bridges' office that very first time was the worst mistake of our lives." He paused for another moment. "I won't lie to you—I've never felt such intense hatred for anyone else in this world. My Mel was dead in the ground and this doctor who put her there was going about his life like nothing happened. Mel obviously wasn't a human being to him; she was just another one of his cases. I drove around for hours thinking and reliving until I couldn't take it anymore. I knew I had to end it that night once and for all. So, with my handgun in the glove compartment, I drove to Bridges' office. I'd remembered he once mentioned that he usually worked late on weeknights and I was hoping with everything inside of me that when I reached he'd be there. And to my relief, his car was still in the parking lot."

"How'd you get in the building?"

"The main door was unlocked, so I walked right in," Todd said. "The bastard was obviously too cheap to hire security to be there with him when he was working late."

"When you got inside, where was Doctor Bridges?"

"He was in his office. That's where I shot him."

"Did he say anything to you when he saw you? Kenna probed.

"I can't remember. All I remember was pulling the trigger."

Kenna studied him. "What did you do afterwards?"

"I hurried back to my car," Todd said. "Then I drove to the Killarney River where I tossed the gun. I knew with the strong current there it would probably never be found. That's about the size of it, Detective."

"Thank you for your statement, Mister Robinson. A typed confession containing these details you've just provided will be prepared for you to sign." Kenna started to get up. "I'll be back when it's ready."

"Okay."

Kenna left the room and quickly made her way to the adjacent room where her partner was.

"What a story, huh?" Jackson said after she walked in.

"I was in there feeling sorry for the guy." Kenna sighed. "Had to keep reminding myself that he was a killer regardless of his motives."

"Something doesn't feel right though."

She sat down in front of the computer and retrieved the recording, then glanced at Jackson. "This guy was very detailed and everything he said was convincing enough for me. If there's more to this story, I'd be shocked. We can get the guys out there to start searching for the gun, but we've got a solid confession, so we'd hardly need it."

Jackson was doubtful.

"I need to send this recording to the front to get his statement prepared."

12

"There's absolutely nothing we can do," Jim Cruz, an attorney and member of the local parish told Joe who was standing in his office, along with Agatha.

"What do you mean there's nothing you can do?" Joe asked, incredulously.

"Todd Robinson confessed to the crime and has refused legal counsel."

"That bastard!" Agatha snarled. "Why would he do a stupid thing like that?"

"Maybe because he's guilty…" Jim returned. "Guilty or a wacko."

"He's not guilty," Joe said. "But I'm beginning to think he may be the other word, albeit temporarily." Then he had a thought. "Hey…can't we use that as the basis to get him evaluated?"

"You mean…by a shrink?" Jim sought clarification.

"Yes."

"Definitely! And if he's found to be mentally unstable, his confession could possibly be declared invalid."

"Now, you're speaking my language!" Joe said.

"But you're not his attorney, Jim, so how can you request a mental evaluation of him?"

"Because according to the law books in this fine city, any member of the public of sound mind can request that on behalf of someone who has confessed to a heinous crime and is in police custody. However, they must make a strong argument for it," Jim said. "That's where I come in."

Agatha was hopeful.

"The boy needs help, Jim. Let's help him," Joe said.

"Whatever you say, Father." Jim nodded.

"Come on, Agatha. We've got our own work to do." Joe headed for the door.

* * * *

Agatha soon noticed that they weren't headed in the direction of the church and Joe wasn't saying anything.

"Where are we going, Father?" she asked as he drove along the thoroughfare.

"We're going to try and find the real killer," he replied. "There are still a couple more suspects on the list that I haven't crossed off."

"What list?"

"It's a long story, Agatha."

"Have you been doing some investigating of your own before they arrested Todd?" she asked. "Oh! I remember! That's why you wanted Beulah to give you a call."

"I've been doing what I can," he said.

Agatha smiled. "That's really admirable of you, Father."

"I just go where the Lord leads me." He made a left turn through Silver Meadows subdivision, an upscale neighborhood on the western side of town.

A few minutes later, they pulled up in front of a white two-story home surrounded by a white wall. Joe noticed that there was no gate in front.

"What should I do?" Agatha asked nervously as they were getting out of the car.

"Stand there and look like a good Christian," Joe answered.

After having made their way to the front cherry-stained double doors, Joe pressed the doorbell and they waited.

Moments later, a thin man about his forties, medium height and of West Indian origin opened the door. He was dressed in a grey suit and tie and a black vest.

"May I help you?" he asked.

Joe wondered if he was the butler.

"Yes. Good afternoon, sir. I am Father Joe McCullen and with me here is Agatha Hall. We are from Saint John's Cathedral."

"Yes…?"

"Is this Mrs. Fiona Wright's residence?" Joe asked.

"It is," the man affirmed.

"We were wondering if we might be able to have a brief word with her."

"Please…come right in." He stepped aside.

Agatha glanced at Joe who was smiling. He was surprised to have been invited right in without a slew of questions being thrown at them

123

first. Some of the other persons he'd attempted to visit whose names were on the list didn't care if he was a priest or a hamster and he'd even gotten the door slammed in his face a couple of times.

"What a lovely home!" Joe exclaimed as they were being led across the large, spacious great room.

"By the way, I am Brian Bakshi, Mrs. Wright's guardian," the man announced. "She always appreciates when members of the clergy stop by to offer prayer."

"Very good." Joe smiled even more widely. There lay the answer to their immediate invitation.

Agatha was also smiling, trying her best to *look like a good Christian*, as the priest had put it. She wasn't sure if having the smile stretched across her face the entire time would be serving the purpose. However, she deemed it was better than appearing nonchalant or annoyed which would definitely draw a negative light.

They climbed the beautiful spiral staircase situated toward the rear of the ground floor and soon entered the first bedroom on the right side of the hallway. Everything about the house was immaculate and the antique furniture everywhere gave the house a luxurious feel.

Brian lightly knocked on the open door, then entered the room. Joe and Agatha followed. The bedroom had beige-colored walls and thick, white curtains at the windows which partly slumped onto the carpeted floor.

Sixty-year-old Fiona Wright was sitting in a red leather chair near the bed with a folded cover resting on her legs. Her disfigured face came as a shock to Joe and Agatha but they were successful in not showing it.

Is this another one of Doctor Bridges' handiwork? Joe instantly wondered.

"Fiona, this is Father Joe from Saint John's and…" He'd clearly forgotten Agatha's name.

"Agatha Hall, ma'am," she said.

Fiona nodded.

"They're here to spend a little time with you today."

He turned to Joe and Agatha. "Please have a seat." He glanced in the direction of two chairs in front of Fiona's which were identical to the one she was sitting in.

It was clear to Joe that they'd arranged the room in such a manner where Fiona's visitors could be accommodated.

"May I offer you something to drink?" Brian asked them.

"No. Thank you," they both replied.

"Okay. Fiona, I'll be in the kitchen if you need anything."

He then left the room.

"How are you today, Mrs. Wright?" Joe asked, tenderly.

"Good! Good!" Her words were muffled as her mouth was slightly curled upwards.

"That's wonderful to hear! Would you like for us to pray with you?" Joe asked.

"Yes!" She quickly nodded.

They all bowed their heads and Joe led the prayer.

"Dear Lord, we come before you today with grateful hearts for all you have bestowed upon us. We ask that you forgive us our sins and continue to lead and guide us in our daily walk and to be an inspiration to others. We ask you to bless Sister Fiona and to keep her strong and grounded in the faith and that all of her needs

will be met. In the name of the Father, and of the Son, and of the Holy Spirit."

There was a collective *Amen.*

"Thank you." Fiona smiled at them both, although her once beautiful smile was barely evident.

Agatha glanced at Joe, wondering when he was going to get to the real purpose of their visit. But instead, he went on to ask Fiona how her day was going, then he talked about the weather and the church, among other things. A half hour later, they were bidding Fiona goodbye and Joe was promising to return for prayer and more good conversation.

As they followed Brian through the great room again, Agatha nudged Joe.

With a gesture of his hand, he urged her to relax.

"Thank you so much for coming," Brian said at the door after he'd shown them out.

"It was indeed a pleasure." Joe replied, standing on the porch. "Mrs. Wright is a wonderful soul."

"Yes, she is," Brian agreed.

"Do you mind sharing what happened to her?" he asked.

Brian stepped out onto the porch with them and eased the door shut.

"I really don't like to talk about this in Fiona's presence," he said quietly. "It's such a dreadful memory of hers. Yet, it's not so much of a memory since she has to live with it every day."

Joe and Agatha were listening attentively.

"What happened is that she went to a doctor across town who was supposed to do a cosmetic procedure on her to correct a part of her face that was slightly disfigured due to a disease she suffered with. Of course, he came highly recommended and Fiona always made pertinent decisions based on recommendations."

Joe and Agatha both nodded.

"Well, making a long story short, this doctor apparently went berserk with the knife while she was on the operating table and when it was all said and done, dear Fiona was worse off than she'd been before. When confronted about it, he, of course, denied any wrongdoing and said that no surgery is promised to be a raving success. He and I had a few words right there in his office and I must admit that I said some things that I'm not proud of, Father, but I was very upset. Fiona is a wonderful, giving, compassionate lady and she didn't deserve to be meddled with like that."

"I'm so sorry to hear that," Joe said.

"Ever since, she's refused to go anywhere other than to her doctor—a general practitioner she's known for years."

"Would you mind revealing who the doctor was who performed her surgery?" Joe probed.

"I don't mind at all. It was Doctor Mark Bridges—the man found dead in his office just recently. I must confess, I wasn't too shocked when I heard the news. I told the detectives investigating his case the same thing when they came by a couple of weeks after his death. The exchange I had in his office that day was heated, but for goodness's sake, as uncaring as he was, I didn't wish the man that sort of harm."

"Thank you for sharing that with us, Brian," Joe said. "We will keep you and Mrs. Wright in our prayers. You both have experienced quite an ordeal."

"Yes, Father, I would appreciate that. And feel free to stop by again whenever you can. Fiona would be ever so grateful."

Brian reentered the house after Joe and Agatha arrived at the car.

"Nice man," Agatha noted as they drove off.

"A real gentleman."

"Who might be the killer…" she added.

"He had nothing to do with it," Joe said.

"How do you know, Father? We mustn't be naïve about this. The Lord said they come as wolves in sheep's clothing."

"And, of course, I agree, but the man is innocent."

"How could you possibly know that?" Agatha exclaimed.

"I have a feeling about these things, Agatha. Don't forget—we came here wondering if Mrs. Wright was the guilty party, but obviously, she couldn't have possibly harmed Doctor Bridges nor anyone else. Not in the state she's in. Sometimes, things are not what they seem."

Agatha was quiet.

"Trust me on this. As we cross more and more people off, the list of potential suspects is getting shorter and we're getting closer to the killer."

"Yes, Father."

<u>13</u>

---

he next day..

"We've filed a motion with the court to have Todd evaluated by a psychiatrist," Jim Cruz told Joe at the rectory.

"That's good. When will we get word on it?" Joe asked.

"As soon as possible. Right now, his confession has been placed on hold until a decision comes back from Judge Carter."

"So far, so good. Let's pray for the best."

"Yes, Father."

"I tried to see Todd today, but they have him in solitary confinement due to some altercation he got into," Joe said. "I can only hope he's not been wounded."

"I can get someone on the inside to check on him. I would've been able to get there myself if he didn't have a ban on attorneys." He shrugged.

Joe poured out two glasses of white wine. "It's truly amazing what Todd's had to endure this year." He handed Jim his glass then sat at the table with him. "First, having to watch Melanie suffer through a terrible illness, eventually losing her and now this. But the Lord would not put more on us than we can bear. We must continue to trust in His mercy."

"Yep." Jim took a sip of the wine.

"Some things are hard to understand in this life, even for me. And I'm the one who's supposed to see the bright side of everything and be a source of strength for others. But sometimes, it can really be overwhelming."

Jim leaned forward. "You've been doing your own investigation into this case. Haven't you, Father?"

"I've been trying to help an innocent man—a man who is hellbent on destroying himself," Joe replied.

"But why are you getting yourself so deeply entangled into this whole matter? From what you said, you don't even know him that well."

"I know enough," Joe replied. "And I made a promise to his wife. Melanie would've never imagined her Todd would've been embroiled in a murder case. And she certainly wouldn't have approved of what he's doing now. He's just been so muleheaded since her passing. Nothing the man does seem to make sense. I know he blames himself for her death, but he's taken his guilt to a whole new level to where it doesn't make sense." He took a sip of his wine. "Who would want to spend possibly the rest of their life in prison for a crime they didn't commit?"

"A person who's in deep despair, I suppose," Jim said. "A person who feels hopeless—like life has no meaning anymore."

Joe nodded. "That's what I should be saying to you, Jim. You see? I'm not as smart or as wise as some people think." Joe felt a bit foolish.

"Don't fool yourself, Father," Jim quickly replied. "I only said that because I know how Todd feels. Never mind what I said earlier. I've been there to the brink of despair after our daughter Ava died."

"Yes, I remember."

"After the accident, I didn't know what to do with myself. I felt like I'd betrayed my little girl who only got to live six years on this earth," Jim said, sadly. "It was my job to protect her; I'm her father. But although I was driving and she had nothing to do with us being on the road that night, I was the one that lived and she died. You don't how many times I replayed that night in my head and how many times I was tempted to end my own life. Guilt and grief are a horrible combination, Father. If it weren't for my wife's constant encouragement and support, and the counseling you selflessly provided as much as I needed it, I wouldn't be sitting here with you right now. So, when you talk about not being as smart and wise as people think you are—you're wrong. You're the smartest, wisest man I've ever met and you've made a tremendous difference in the lives of countless people out there. When you have your moments thinking you're not worthy of the task, remember me—remember my Ava and remember all the people out there who are alive today and thriving because you helped them."

Joe's eyes were welling with tears and he quickly threw up a hand to dry them.

"Thank you, Jim," he said. "It means a lot."

14

The past few months on the island was like paradise on earth for Cherry Granger. She and James were inseparable and had been spending every moment of their spare time together. Cherry had finally decided to take him across town to meet her relatives and was apprehensive about it during the drive.

"Why are you so nervous?" James asked.

"Because you don't know my family," she replied.

He laughed. "If they're anything like you—even in the slightest, I know I'll love them and we'll get along just fine."

"Don't hold your breath, James. Trust me—you don't know what you're getting into."

"From what you told me, your Aunt Richa and Uncle Paul sound like good people. After I meet them, I'd be happy to meet your other relatives who live nearby."

"We're not doing all of that today. Aunt Richa and Uncle Paul are enough for one day."

He glanced at her from behind the steering wheel of his Jeep. "You've gotta be kidding!"

James followed a dirt track on the right just off the main road and they travelled another minute or two before arriving at a wooden house, seemingly in the back of nowhere.

"This is it," Cherry said as she unfastened her seatbelt.

James stepped out of the vehicle and immediately hurried around to open the door for her.

"Hey, Lucy!" Cherry bent down and hugged the Doberman that ran up to her. "I've missed you so much!" She kissed the animal all over its face.

James smiled. "See—someone here's surely nice. He has no idea who I am and isn't barking at me. That's a good sign."

"That's a trap!" Cherry exclaimed, standing again.

An old couple stepped outside onto the front porch.

"Auntie Richa and Uncle Paul!" Cherry cried from the vicinity of the Jeep.

"Is that you, Cherry?" The woman's eyes lit up. She had long silver hair that dangled midway to her back.

"Yes!" She ran over to them and the three embraced.

"I was wondering what was taking you so long to get here," Richa said. "Last I heard, you moved back to Cayman months ago!"

"I was just getting settled into my new place, Auntie."

"You're all settled in now?" Paul asked.

"Yes, sir," she replied.

"Hi, there." James interjected with a smile.

Paul looked his way as if he just noticed someone standing there. "Who the hell is this?" he asked Cherry.

"Oh! I'm sorry!" She quickly took James' hand. "This is my boyfriend James."

"Boyfriend?" Richa grimaced. "We haven't known you to have any boyfriend since the day you were born."

Cherry was clearly embarrassed.

"Well, it's about time!" Paul said. "Come inside—unless you want a tan out here."

James and Cherry followed the couple inside. James looked at Cherry and raised an eyebrow.

"I told you so," she whispered.

In the living room, Paul went to his rocking chair. Richa picked up a yellow ball of yarn with a needle and sat on the sofa, and Cherry and James sat across from them on the couch.

"So, how's the new house?" Richa asked Cherry as she started to crotchet.

"It's perfect, Auntie. The beach is right behind it too, so I get a good swim at least a couple times a week."

"Yeah. Keep getting into that salt water as much as possible," Paul told her. "I told you and your cousins countless times it has healing properties. I get a dip myself every weekday morning and I keep telling this old woman to come, but she's as stubborn as an ox."

"He's just trying to live longer." Richa winked. "But I told him it's useless. When his time is up…it's up."

"Stupid talk!" Paul murmured.

Cherry and James chuckled.

Paul soon looked at James. "So, what do you want with my niece?" he asked.

"Uncle!" Cherry exclaimed.

"Not you, Cherry," Paul said. "I'm speaking to James here. We're having a man-to-man conversation."

Cherry glanced at her aunt who'd made eye contact then continued to crochet.

"Well—I asked a question!" Paul barked.

"Cherry is very special to me," James replied, calmly. "We've just been dating for a short time, but I feel like I've known her all my life." He looked into Cherry's eyes. "I'm in love with her."

"Yeah—that's what they all say," Paul scoffed. "Nice words don't move me, young man. I'm too old and too irritated to be fooled."

"Well…" James wasn't sure of what else to say.

"James is wonderful man, Uncle Paul," Cherry said. "And he's treated me like a queen ever since the day we met."

"Where did y'all meet?" Richa asked.

"We met at the pub," Cherry replied.

"You mean the pub my brother gave you?"

140

"Yes."

"I was talking to her for the longest time before I learned that she was the owner," James indicated.

"Maybe that's what you want with her." Richa looked him dead in the eyes.

"No, it's not!" Cherry rebutted. "James is a pilot and he has his own charter company. You can barely compare that to an old pub."

"Did any of you understand what I meant about me and James here having a man-to-man conversation?" Paul soon interjected.

The room suddenly went silent.

"I asked what you wanted with my niece and you gave me some fairytale story," he told James. "What you own doesn't impress me. Where you came from doesn't impress me. What matters is what your intentions are and that way, I know who you are as a man."

"Fair enough." James nodded.

He then slipped something out of his pocket and turned to Cherry. "When you told me last week that we were coming here so that I can meet two of the most important people in your life, I decided to hold off asking you to marry me until we got here."

Completely shocked, Cherry covered her mouth with her hands and tears began to well in her eyes.

Richa's face softened as she looked on and Paul's expression was unreadable.

James got down on one knee in front of Cherry and opened the tiny box. He took her hand into his and said, "Cherry Granger...I would be honored to spend the rest of my life with you. Will you marry me?"

Tears now streaming down her face, she quickly nodded. "Yes! Yes, I'll marry you!"

He slid the large diamond ring onto her finger, then rose to his feet and sat down again. The two of them embraced tightly.

"I guess you got your answer, old man," Richa told her husband.

"I guess I did!" Paul stood up and instinctively, James did too.

"Welcome to the family!" Paul extended his hand.

"Thank you," James replied with a smile and the men shook hands vigorously.

Richa went over and hugged her niece, then hugged James.

"Congratulations to you kids," she said.

James and Cherry spent another hour with them and James was amazed at how quickly Paul had warmed up to him. He actually seemed like a great guy.

Occasionally, during the drive back home, Cherry found herself in tears. She could barely keep her eyes off the ring.

"I can't believe you did that…and in front of them!" she cried.

James chuckled.

"When you got down on your knees to propose, I wondered if I was dreaming."

"It was no dream, honey." He gently squeezed her knee. "I wanted to propose a week after we met, but I knew I'd come across as a nut, so I patiently waited for the right time."

"A week after we'd met?" She grimaced. "You're right—I would've taken you for a nut and probably run for the hills."

"You don't believe in love at first sight?" he asked.

"I do, but I don't believe in marriage proposals after one week! That's insane. Just my opinion. What can someone know about a person in one week? Close to nothing!"

James smiled. "That's why I held back. From the basis of this conversation, I'm glad I did."

15

Two weeks later…

After some digging of his own and further consulting with Jim Cruz's PI—Donald Angler—Joe was able to locate twenty-eight-year-old Ian Miller at a homeless shelter a couple of blocks away from the church. Ian stood at six feet tall and weighed two hundred and thirty pounds. He had blonde hair and blue eyes.

"Mister Miller, it's a pleasure to meet you," Joe said as they shook hands. "You're a hard man to track down."

They proceeded to walk along the embankment behind the shelter.

"Maybe because I've had enough years to master the art of disappearing." Ian shoved his hands into his pockets. "You mentioned you're looking for some information about the doc someone killed a couple of months ago."

"I am," Joe replied.

"What makes you think I can help you with that?" Ian asked. "I told the cops everything I know—which is nothing much."

"You used to be a patient of Doctor Bridges?"

"A couple of years ago." He sighed heavily.

"Can you tell me more about it? Whatever you can share would be greatly appreciated."

"If you're trying to find out if I had anything to do with his death, you're wasting your time," Ian told him. "Our relationship came to an end just as quickly as it got started."

"Relationship?" Joe was confused.

Ian stopped walking, picked up a few pebbles and tossed them into the water. He then brushed his hands off on the leg of his pants.

"Mark and I had a brief affair when I was a patient there. I actually met him at his office when I had issues swallowing due to some excessive postnasal drip."

"Did he help you with that?" Joe asked.

"Surely did. He checked things out and in no time had me back to normal again. As far as the relationship went, he treated me really well.

Bought me a car, paid my apartment rent and gave me whatever I needed. The problem came when, I guess, I started to want more than he was willing or able to give."

"You mean…you two had some kind of a falling out?"

"A *falling out* is putting it mildly." He laughed. "All hell broke loose is more like it! See, Father…up to the time my mom died, I was pretty used to getting my way."

"Some people will call that *spoiled*," Joe said.

"Undoubtedly, I was! If someone told me I couldn't have something I wanted, there was usually hell to pay!" He noticed the priest's altered expression. "I must say I've changed a lot over the past year though. I've been getting some free counseling right there at the shelter. A shrink comes by once a week and I never fail to make use of her services."

"That's good, Mister Miller. Sounds like you're on the right track."

"Please call me, Ian. *Mister Miller* makes me sound old." He cringed.

Joe smiled.

"Well, the bottom line as far as Mark and I are concerned is that he eventually broke up with me because he said I was too needy. And I didn't know how to handle that."

"So, what did you do?" Joe was curious.

"I went to his office the next morning, raised Cain in front of everybody, trashed the place as much as I could before the cops got there, then got my ah…I mean…*behind* thrown in jail. He didn't press charges though. I'm guessing because he didn't want this thing blowing up any more than it had. He offered me an apology and some cash to move on and keep my mouth shut. And scared to end up in the slammer again, I accepted his measly five thousand dollars and went my way," Ian explained. "In no time, I was out of work, out of cash and got kicked out of my apartment. I lived in my car for a while until I sold it to support my drug habit. Yeah—the one I took up after the failed relationship. I'm clean now though; stopped cold turkey on my own and working on getting my life together."

Joe admired his determination.

"You're a strong young man." He patted Ian on the back. "You can do anything you put your mind to. And as long as you keep your focus on the straight and narrow path, you'll have good success in this life."

"Thank you, Father. I hope I was able to help in some way," Ian said.

"You have. Look—if you ever need food or counseling, or help getting back on your feet, you can always come by Saint John's, just a couple of blocks away from here. We'd be happy to assist."

"I appreciate that, Father," the young man said.

As Joe headed back to his car, he knew that Ian Miller would be the next name he crossed off the list. And he was beginning to really get worried.

There was no one left to locate.

* * * *

"How are you holding up?" Joe asked Todd.

They were sitting at a table in the visiting room of the prison. Todd was not at all the man Joe remembered. A matter of a few months and undoubtedly, a lot of emotional turmoil had dramatically altered his appearance and he looked both mentally and physically unhealthy.

"I'm great!" Todd replied, smiling.

Joe studied his face, hoping to find some inkling of the old Todd there. "Why don't you stop this, Todd? If you can't for yourself, why don't you do it for Mel? You know she never would've approved of what you're doing."

"What am I doing, Father?"

Joe leaned in. "Sabotage. You're sabotaging your life; giving it up for what you think is a worthy cause, but it's not. Confessing to a murder you didn't commit is not a worthy cause, Todd. You know that."

"I bet you and Agatha had something to do with them setting my confession aside and having me see a shrink for some sort of evaluation. But you're wasting your time. I'll have you know that. Furthermore, I need you two to stop meddling in my life. I don't need you and any lawyer. I need to be left alone." He paused for a second. "You think you know me, Father, but you don't. You have no idea who I am. You've seen me at church a few times and that's it. How can you be so convinced that I'm not guilty and why do you even care? Oh—I forgot—it's because of Mel. The truth is you don't know what Mel and I really went through all those months. You *think* you do, but you don't. You heard what we told you, but you didn't live it. That butcher of a doctor cost Mel her life and I finally came clean to the cops and confessed to the crime. I'm sorry I lied to you when we discussed it at the house, but sometimes you have to swallow your pride and tell the truth. And that's what I've done. Now, if you and Agatha and whoever else want to keep thinking that I'm this grieving widower who's falsely confessed to murder, that's on you guys. My conscience is clean and I accept my fate—whatever it is."

Joe was dumbfounded by Todd's refusal to even consider any alternative. It was clear to him now that for Todd, there was no turning back—certainly if his fate was left to him.

* * * *

"What are we gonna do?" Agatha whispered loudly as she sat across from Joe inside of his office. Virginia and Kate were out front working and she didn't want them to

151

overhear their conversation. "Todd's in prison wasting away while the real culprit's out there!"

"The good news is that he's been granted a psychological evaluation—thanks to Jim," Joe said.

"Does that mean they'll let Todd out of prison and send him instead to a mental health facility?"

"No." Joe shook his head. "It means that a psychiatrist appointed by the government will meet with him at the prison a few times to determine if he's in the right frame of mind to offer any confession, considering his recent loss. If he's found not to be, his confession will be thrown out altogether and he'll be made to stand trial."

"How can that be beneficial?" Agatha asked. "He's just gonna say the same thing in court that he said to the detectives that day. He'll simply confess all over again!" She threw her hands up in frustration.

"The good thing about him being made to stand trial would be that we'd have a chance to hopefully shine light upon the fact that Todd's not speaking truthfully about the murder. Once that doubt is planted in the minds of the jury, there's a chance that it will result in an acquittal."

"Or a hung jury," she added.

"Let's hope it's the former—if it even goes that far," Joe replied. "If the confession stands as it is now, we know for sure that Todd's staying in jail probably for the rest of his life. He stands a better chance going on trial."

"But I imagine we'll have a roadblock proving anything if Todd still refuses legal counsel."

"Jim mentioned that he may be able to persuade the judge to allow him to have a *private* psychological evaluation done of Todd pro bono which is bound to work for Todd's benefit, but there's no guarantee that his request will be granted."

Agatha shook her head.

"There's a piece missing from this puzzle, Agatha," Joe stared into space. "The thought keeps nudging at me. I must find out what that piece is."

16

*U*pon completion of a psychiatric evaluation, Todd Robinson's murder confession was set aside and declared void. He was unsuccessful in convincing the psychiatrist that grieving the loss of his wife was not the contributing factor in him rendering a confession, neither to participating in the public desecration of the doctor's grave. The psychiatrist further noted that the validity of any confession he would make with regards to the murder would need to be determined upon examination and cross examination at trial. Ultimately, Todd was deemed competent to stand trial for the murder of Dr. Mark Bridges.

* * * *

One month later…

Cherry Granger was sitting on the couch with her eyes glued to the television screen.

"What is it?" James asked curiously from the kitchen.

"It's that guy—Mister Robinson," Cherry said. "His wife used to be a patient of ours. She died and now he's on trial for murdering my boss."

"Sounds like a soap opera to me," he said.

"Yeah—except it's real. I'm surprised the media over here has picked up this story."

"It's not every day you hear a doctor was murdered and by the husband of a patient—*allegedly*," James said.

Todd was seen on television being escorted to the courthouse in handcuffs and leg shackles. Father Joe McCullen was standing on the pathway leading into the court as Todd passed by with two armed police officers.

"Do you think he did it?" James asked Cherry.

She shook her head. "I don't. He was such a good husband and a good man. I felt like I knew that couple so well all those months they were coming to see Doctor Bridges."

He entered the living room and handed her a ham and cheese sandwich. "Enough of the news!" He picked up the remote after noticing how sad she'd become. "Want me to look for a game show or something?"

"I guess," she answered, sliding over to make room for him.

* * * *

Despite all of his own supporters' efforts, Todd still fiercely resisted having any legal representation. Camila Bridges sat in the courtroom with friends and relatives who were eager to see him pay for the murder of their loved one.

Detectives Jackson and Kenna were also present and were seated at the back of the room. Joe and Agatha were on the opposite side of the Bridges' family in the middle row.

"Mister Robinson," Judge Irene Keesh started. "I understand that you have refused the representation of an attorney. Is that correct?"

"That is correct, Your Honor," Todd replied, standing.

"It is incumbent upon me to advise you that your decision to reject legal counsel is not a smart one and I would strongly urge you to reconsider. If you cannot afford an attorney, one will be appointed for you by the court."

"I stand by my decision, Your Honor."

"So be it," Keesh replied.

Hope Harman, the prosecuting attorney, was a middle-aged woman with short, black curly hair and a round face. She stood at four feet five inches tall and had graduated with top honors from her law school. She had a reputation of bringing more than ninety percent of the persons she prosecuted to justice and although well sought after by private law firms, she had declined every offer.

Hope was a victim of crime herself. She had been abducted as a child and hidden from her family for three months by a deranged child molester—only found when the perpetrator was reported by a neighbor to police for screams coming from his basement. She was just eight years old when it happened. That experience fueled for Hope a desire for justice and she was determined to spend her life getting as many criminals off the streets as she possibly could.

She started with a powerful opening argument that painted Todd Robinson as a man who'd lost complete control and was a danger to society.

Todd listened quietly, unbothered by the way she'd portrayed him. In fact, he appeared quite relaxed.

Judge Keesh glanced over at him several times wondering what might have been going through his mind. A pro bono private psychiatric evaluation was presented to her court by the Law Offices of Jim Cruz & Co without the consent of the accused and Keesh felt she had no choice but to reject it.

Heather Caddel was the first witness called to the stand and Nurse June Mortimer would be next. Hope Harman expected the ladies to share with the court the explosive confrontation between Todd and Dr. Bridges shortly before Melanie Robinson passed away.

Heather clearly didn't want to be on the stand that day. As far as she was concerned, Bridges had brought the murder upon himself. The only thing she was annoyed about was the fact that she was now out of a job.

"Heather Caddel, do you vow to tell the truth, the whole truth and nothing but the truth, so help you God?" The bailiff asked her as she raised her right hand.

"I do," she responded.

Hope Harman asked her to tell the court how she came to know Todd Robinson.

"His wife was Doctor Bridges' patient and he was with her for every visit," she answered.

"What type of man did you find him to be?"

Quiet, pleasant— for the most part."

"When you say *for the most part*, what do you mean?" Harman asked.

"He was nice. His wife Melanie was more talkative with the staff than he was, but he was a pleasant person," Heather explained.

"I see. In the months leading up to Doctor Bridges' murder, would you say that Mister Robinson was still nice and pleasant?"

Heather glanced over at Todd who was just twiddling his thumbs.

"Well, he seemed more agitated after a while, but that's only because…"

159

"Did he seem very upset at Doctor Bridges?"

"Not the whole while. Mostly towards the end."

Harman glanced at her notes, then asked, "To the best of your knowledge…what was Mister Robinson upset about?"

"To my understanding, he blamed Doctor Bridges for misleading them regarding his wife's condition for the sake of making money. He also blamed him for doing a bad job with the procedures he performed on Mrs. Robinson," Heather explained.

Harman made a few steps across the front of the courtroom.

"Miss Caddel, did you see any signs that Mister Robinson was becoming unhinged in the weeks or months leading up to the doctor's murder?"

"Unhinged?"

"Yes. Mentally disturbed."

"I wouldn't say that," Heather replied. She looked Todd's way again. "To me, he appeared more disappointed and sad than anything else."

Moments later, Harman asked, "Did you ever hear Todd Robinson threaten Doctor Bridges in any way?"

"I'm not sure I would call what I heard a threat."

"May I remind you, Miss Caddel, that you have sworn an oath to tell the truth to this honorable court."

"Thanks for the reminder, but I am very aware of that and have told the truth," Heather said matter-of-factly.

"Again, I ask you…did you ever hear Todd Robinson threaten Doctor Bridges in any way?"

Joe and Sue glanced at each other. They could feel the intensity of the examination. Harman was clearly not an easy woman to handle, but neither was Heather.

"The answer is *No*." Heather looked the prosecutor directly in her eyes. "I never heard Mister Robinson threaten Doctor Bridges."

Harman sighed. "What did you hear Todd Robinson say to Doctor Bridges approximately two weeks before the doctor was murdered?"

"I heard Mister Robinson tell Doctor Bridges that he will pay for what he did to Mrs. Robinson and so will his two children."

"And you didn't take that as a threat, Miss Caddel?" Harman pressed.

"No, I didn't. At least, not in the way that you mean it. I also heard Mister Robinson tell Doctor Bridges that he was a man of faith and that he would reap what he'd sown. Sounded to me like he meant that God would get Doctor Bridges, not that Mister Robinson would kill him."

Joe was nodding, happily.

"That girl doesn't play," he whispered to Agatha.

"She surely doesn't."

Heather was soon allowed to leave the stand and she quickly made her way out of the courtroom.

Nurse June Mortimer was called to the stand next.

Agatha leaned in. "Father, you do know that if Todd is found guilty, he may face a harsher sentence than what might've been offered to him when he confessed, right?"

"I'm aware of that," he answered.

As she was speaking, Joe was scrolling through his phone's calendar.

"With Jim's private psychiatric proposal being rejected by the judge it seems like we don't have a leg to stand on. There's nothing more we can do for him," Agatha continued.

Joe was silent when suddenly, an idea struck him.

"Where are you going?" she asked as he started to get up.

"Outside to use the phone. Stay here."

He headed out into the courtyard and sat down with his phone in hand. "Lord, if I'm wrong, please stop me," he whispered.

He made a call to Donald Angler, who answered on the first ring. "Don, I have a hunch. I need some information," Joe told him.

Donald listened carefully to what Joe had said, then promptly went to work.

Forty-five minutes later, he called back. "It's just as you suspected, Father. Be careful."

Joe drove to a subdivision called Fairland Terrace and three streets from the main road was Tucker Street. He took a left turn there, then drove a short distance until he came upon a little blue house, which from the overgrown yard, appeared uninhabited.

Joe got out of his car and proceeded to walk up to the yard. The windows were shielded by sheets of plywood and a two-by-four had been placed across the front door.

Upon glancing around, Joe got the impression that it was a fairly quiet neighborhood. A few children were spotted further up the street in front of a house playing hopscotch.

He stood in front of the house wondering why he'd felt such an urge to go there when there was clearly nothing remarkable to see. He soon made his way around the house paying close attention to his surroundings, particularly the structure itself since it was nearly impossible to inspect the yard due to the overgrown weeds.

"This is stupid," he muttered as he eventually headed back around to the front of the house again. "I just wasted my time and gas coming out here walking around this house like a fool."

Then suddenly, at the side of the porch near a cluster of wilted tulips, he noticed something poking out from a small concrete opening. He quickly went over and stooped down next to it, and while sliding it out, his eyes widened with shock.

"Finally—the missing piece of the puzzle," he said.

* * * *

Cherry was at the pub that day when her cell phone rang. She noticed the call was from a private number.

Stepping just outside of the door, she answered it.

"Cherry...it's Father Joe. How are you?"

"I'm fine, Father! How are you?" She wasn't sure what to make of the sound of his voice.

"I found it, Cherry," he said. "You need to come home."

Just then, her heart sank to the floor and her stomach felt loose.

---

17

*C*herry drove to James' house after he returned home from his last flight that afternoon.

James lived in a ten thousand square foot home surrounded by glass windows which offered a tantalizing view of the massive pool outside and a beautifully manicured lawn. Cherry had planned to move there in three months' time after their wedding.

"There's something I need to tell you," she said to him as they sat in the living room together.

He noticed the look of angst on her face and was immediately concerned. "What's the matter, honey?"

He drew closer to her on the sofa and suddenly, she felt unable to speak. In a split second, by means of a phone call, her entire life had been altered and there was nothing she could do about it.

He gently lifted her chin and forced her to meet his gaze. "You can tell me anything," he said softly.

"I'm not the woman that you think I am." She was looking into his eyes and wondering if that would be the final time.

"What are you talking about? Of course, you are. I've always been a good judge of character." He smiled.

"I'm not kidding, James." She turned away momentarily, then set her focus on those loving eyes of his again. "What I'm about to say will ruin everything and before I even say it, I want you to know that I'm sorry and I never intended to hurt you. You were the only man that I ever loved in my entire life and I'd come to think that I had been waiting for you all these years without even knowing you existed. Since I came back home, these have been the best few months of my life because I got to spend them with you."

James was confused and more worried than before. "What is it, Cherry?" he asked.

She lowered her head, took a deep breath in, then said, "I killed a man."

"You what?" He grimaced.

"I'm the one that killed my boss—Doctor Bridges."

James sat up straight. "You're kidding, right?"

Cherry shook her head slowly.

"So, the man on TV you told me about who was going to trial for the murder was actually innocent?"

She nodded.

"And you knew that all along because you were the one…"

Again, she nodded.

"But how? Why?" He felt like the world had suddenly crashed around him and he was stuck in a bad dream.

Tears were now welling in her eyes. "I'd had enough. Enough of watching patient after patient come into the office hoping to get the help they needed and leaving distressed—sometimes worse off than they were before and others dying when they had so much life left in them," she said. "I'd befriended many of those people and had come to care about them, but Doctor Bridges didn't ever seem to care. They were just dollar signs to him—opportunities for him to go on more expensive vacations with his family, buy better cars and so forth. To him, they were not human beings with feelings, families, loved ones...or hope. Sometimes things went right, but many times, they went wrong. Why? I'm not sure. When he first started his private practice, it wasn't like that. He was an excellent surgeon. Maybe over the years as the bank accounts grew, he started to care less about his patients and wasn't handling them nor operating on them with the care he once had. I had to sit there and watch him ruin people's lives for so many years. And every time a new person walked in the office for the first time, I wanted so badly to tell them to turn around and to never come back, but I couldn't do it. I needed my job."

"So, you figured to end his reign of terror that you'd murder him?"

"Yes," she said, quietly. "I couldn't bring myself to just pick up and leave and not ensure that others were safe when I went. The probability of more terrible cases arising after my retirement haunted me for months leading up to it and finally I knew that I had to make a decision to end it once and for all."

Shaking his head in disbelief, James felt like the strength had been knocked right out of him.

"I'm really sorry, James. I didn't mean to come into your life and turn it upside down the way I've done. I realize that you would've been better off—*we* would've been better off if we'd never met."

"Don't say that, Cherry, because that's not how I feel."

His response caught her by surprise.

"It's not?" she asked.

"No. But I have to say that although I understand your motivation behind the killing, it doesn't make it right, Cherry. You're not God. You don't have a right to kill anyone. As evil as that man obviously was, he had a family whom I'm sure loved him. Did he have kids?"

"Yes. Two boys," she replied.

"That's what I wish you'd thought about before doing that vigilante stuff. Even though you've saved other people, you've ruined your own life over a man who wasn't even worth it."

She felt his pain as he spoke.

"And you've deprived me of having you with me for the rest of my life," he added. "I take it you've decided to turn yourself in?"

"Yes. Truthfully—not of my own accord," she confessed. "A priest who knows the accused man and his wife found the gun I used to murder Doctor Bridges in a gap on the side of my porch. I guess I didn't hide it well enough before rushing off to the airport that night. The priest advised me to go back to Old Providence and confess what I'd done and he offered to go with me to the police. And that's what I'm gonna do."

James was pondering everything she'd said. "So, what was the final straw?" he asked. "Was it just knowing you were retiring and you didn't want the cycle to continue, like you said or was there a tipping point?"

She nodded quickly. "It was the death of Melanie Robinson."

"You mean—the wife of the man that was accused of the doctor's murder?"

"Yes." She gulped. "Melanie was a wonderful person. She had the most vibrant, caring, positive attitude of any person I ever came across. When she came to the office for the first time, she was so healthy-looking and happy. We chatted a lot; she made jokes and always brought a smile to our faces. My co-workers also loved her. But after seeing Doctor Bridges for a while, everything changed about her. She started to deteriorate and rather quickly. Eventually, the smile had vanished completely and she could no longer speak. Her poor husband was devastated as he watched his wife slowly dying. You don't know how much it hurt me to witness that. It was the reason I'd made up my mind that there was no way I was going to retire and go on to live a beautiful, peaceful life knowing I was leaving a human beast behind to continue on his path of destruction. I just couldn't do it," she explained.

James used his fingers to wipe the tears from her cheeks, then held her close.

"It's okay," he said as she leaned against his chest, sobbing. "I'm right here. Everything's gonna be okay."

hree days later…

At half past eight on Tuesday morning, Cherry Granger walked into the police station with Father Joe McCullen on her right and Beulah Hart on her left. They headed over to the sergeant sitting at the reception desk.

"I'm here to confess to the murder of Doctor Mark Bridges," Cherry announced, holding a paper bag in her hand.

The officer quickly picked up the phone and spoke quietly to the person on the line.

Then moments later, Detective Wendy Kenna approached them.

"Good morning. Please come this way," she said.

Cherry surrendered the handgun used in the killing and upon making a complete confession was booked for murder that morning. Buelah Hart hugged her tightly and said, "It's gonna be all right. Everyone's gonna see you're not a bad person."

With tears streaming down her face, Cherry nodded.

"You did the right thing by coming clean," Joe told her. "Keep the faith; I am praying for you."

She was then escorted to a holding cell.

Todd Robinson was subsequently released from prison and immediately ordered into inpatient grief counseling at a mental health facility on the other side of town.

"You can't let me out of jail!" He went kicking and screaming into the bus that would transport him there. "I killed my wife! I killed her! I deserve to be there!"

His plea fell on deaf ears and he was on his way to the Old Providence Mental Health Facility. Todd was deemed suicidal and placed under twenty-four hours surveillance.

* * * *

"How'd you figure it out?" Sue McCloud asked Joe as she and Agatha sat with him on the front porch of the rectory days later.

Joe was looking straight ahead pondering the events that led to Cherry Granger's recent confession and Todd Robinson's release.

"When Agatha and I were at court..." he started, "...it suddenly dawned on me that Cherry Granger had left for the Cayman Islands the same day that the doctor was killed. She didn't catch a flight earlier that evening as was suspected, but instead her flight was that night at 9:55. The doctor was killed at approximately 7:30, so although it was tight, she had sufficient time to do the deed and then catch her flight. What no one knew was that she had originally planned to leave for Grand Cayman on the 23rd, which would have been four days after her last day on the job. However, she switched her flight to the 19th instead—the day she planned to kill Doctor Bridges. Rushing to catch her flight, she did a poor job of concealing the weapon in a concrete opening of the porch."

"And for purely selfish reasons, she was willing to let an innocent man, whom she claimed to care about, go to prison for the rest of his life," Agatha added.

"Well, the woman just got engaged and was planning a wedding," Joe noted. "I imagine for her it was a struggle. She claimed when she first realized that Todd was actually their prime suspect, she wanted to come forth with the truth, but in the end, she chose her own happiness. She was following the case the entire time." He sighed.

"Wow." Sue leaned back against the wall. "It's really sad what happened to her and Todd. She did the deed believing she could save—God knows how many other people from suffering at the hands of Doctor Bridges. Her motive was pure, but killing the man, unless in self-defense, could never be justified. No one has the right."

"I agree," Joe said.

"Well, I don't!" Agatha stated.

They both looked at her.

"Doctor Bridges destroyed the lives of many innocent people who depended on him to help them and he's responsible for the premature death of one of my dearest friends. Mel was a sweet soul and nothing can ever bring her back. I might look bad for saying this and even feel a little guilty for it, but I'm glad Doctor Bridges is dead. I'm just sorry that he managed to destroy yet another young life by provoking a once law-abiding citizen with such a bright future ahead of her to commit the unthinkable."

For a good while, there was complete silence. They each felt a sense of loss and sadness for the parties involved.

"You know what I can't understand?" Sue soon broke the silence.

"What?" Agatha asked.

"How Todd knew what kind of gun was used to kill the doctor. I don't remember hearing that detail on the news."

"It was a lucky guess," Joe said. "A 357 Magnum is a commonly used weapon and it turns out that it was, in fact, Cherry Granger's weapon of choice for the murder. If Todd's guess was wrong, I'm pretty sure the detectives would've figured out from the get-go that he was lying about even being at Doctor Bridges' office that night. One good guess got him what he wanted—at least for a while until Cherry came forth."

"Amazing." Sue shook her head.

"Well, at least now since Judge Keesh ordered Todd into grief counseling, he's finally getting the help he needs working through the emotions that led him to begin self-destructing in the first place," Agatha said. "So, that's a good thing. My goodness! It was so stressful for us trying to get through to a man who'd already given up on life completely."

"Yep. At least, it's all over now," Joe said. "God works in mysterious ways."

"Yes indeed." Sue nodded in agreement.

~ THE END ~

MURDER AT THE BABY SHOWER - Book 3

in The Joe McCullen Cozy Mystery Series

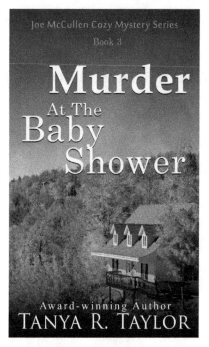

Not everything that glistens in Old Providence is gold.

Victoria Mason has the perfect life - a successful career, a doting husband and now a baby on the way. She'd spent the better part of a decade fixing what had nearly destroyed her and she can now inspire others.

But someone is keeping a dreadful secret that threatens to ruin everything she holds dear.

Will such a secret result in murder? And if so, will it be her own?

VISIT TANYA-R-TAYLOR.COM TO GET IT.

~

MURDER AT THE CONVENT – Book 1 in

The Joe McCullen Cozy Mystery Series

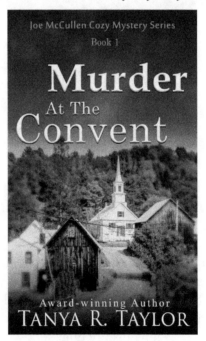

A murdered nun.
A convent full of suspects.
Who could have committed such a
horrible crime?

Father Joe McCullen is no ordinary priest.
He has a heart of gold, but he's no pushover.

Very little passes his ears or his eyes and he can
smell a "rat" from a mile away.

The community of Old Providence is held by
higher standards by the beloved priest, yet
"skeletons" still manage to creep out of the
closets of his faithful parishioners every now and
then, and oftentimes are not headed anywhere in
the direction of the confessional.

Join Father Joe McCullen on the most
extraordinary, eyebrow-raising adventures of
mystery, suspense, humor - and surprise after
surprise!

TANYA-R-TAYLOR.COM

Lucille Pfiffer sees, but not with her eyes. She lives with her beloved dog Vanilla ("Nilla" for short) in a cozy neighborhood that is quite "active" due to what occurred in the distant past. Though totally blind, she plays an integral role in helping to solve pressing and puzzling mysteries, one right after the other, which, without her, might remain unsolved.

The question is: How can she do any of that with such a handicap?

#1 Bestseller and #1 New Release!

FREE EXCERPT:

BLIND SIGHT

Book 1 – Lucille Pfiffer Mystery Series

1

Super Vanilla

I carefully descended the air-conditioned jitney and started down the sidewalk with my cane in hand and Nilla, my pet Shih Tzu on leash at my side. Taking a cab was our preferred mode of transport, but sometimes we enjoyed a nice, long bus ride instead. Nestled on both sides of the street were a number of shops, including convenience stores, jewelry, liquor, antique stores and haberdashery.

It was the day before my scheduled meeting with the local pet society that while walking along downtown Chadsworth, I heard a woman scream. The vision of her anguished face flashed into my mind and the image of a young boy dressed in faded blue jeans and a long-sleeved black shirt running at full speed in the direction Nilla and I were headed. Gripped tightly in his hand was a purse that did not belong to him; his eyes bore a mixture of confidence in his escape intertwined with fear of capture. He was quickly approaching—now only several feet behind us. In no time, he would turn the bend just ahead and be long gone bearing the ill-gotten fruits of his labor.

One could imagine how many times he'd done the same thing and gotten away with it, only to plan his next move – to stealthily lie in wait for his unsuspecting victim. I heard the squish-squashing of his tennis shoes closely behind. It was the precise moment he was about to zoom past us that I abruptly held out my cane to the left, tripping him, and watched as he fell forward, rolling over like a car tire, then ultimately landing flat on his back on the hard pavement. I dropped the leash and yelled, "Get him, Nilla!"

Nilla took off at full speed and pounced on top of the already injured boy, biting him on every spot she could manage – determined to teach him a lesson he'd never forget. He screamed and tried to push her off of him, but a man dashed over and pinned him to the ground. I made my way over to Nilla and managed to get her away from the chaotic scene. Her job was done. As tiny as she was, she made her Momma proud.

The frantic woman got her purse back and the boy was restrained until police arrived.

2

The room was almost packed to capacity when I arrived at the podium with the gracious assistance of a young man. As he went to take his seat in the front row, I proceeded with my introduction: "My name's Lucille Pfiffer—Mrs., that is—even though my husband Donnie has been dead and gone for the past four and a half years now. We had no children, other than our little Shih Tzu, Vanilla; 'Nilla' for short." I smiled, reflectively. "By the way, I must tell you she doesn't respond to 'Nill' or 'Nillie'; it's 'Nilla' if you stand a chance of getting her attention. She totally ignores you sometimes even when you call her by her legal name '*Va (vuh)*...nilla'.

"We reside in a quiet part of town known as Harriet's Cove. A little neighborhood with homes and properties of all sizes. We're mostly middle class folk, pretending to be upper class. The ones with large homes, much bigger than my split level, are the ones you hardly see strolling around the neighborhood, and they certainly don't let their kids play with yours if you've got any. Those kids are the 'sheltered' ones—they stay indoors mainly, other than when it's time to hop in the family car and go wherever for whatever."

I heard the rattle inside someone's throat.

"Uh, Mrs. Pfiffer…" A gentleman at the back of the room stood up. "I don't mean to be rude or anything, but you mentioned the neighbors' kids as if you can see these things you described going on in your neighborhood. I mean, how you said some don't play with others and they only come out when they're about to leave the house. But how do you know any of this? Or should we assume, it's by hearsay?"

I admired his audacity to interrupt an old lady while she's offering a requested and well-meaning introduction to herself. After all, I was a newbie to the Pichton Pet Society and their reputation for having some 'snobby' members preceded them.

"Thank you very much, sir, for the questions you raised," I answered. "Yes, you are to assume that I know some of this—just some—via hearsay. The rest I know from living in my neck of the woods for the past thirty-five years. I haven't always been blind, you know." I liked how they put you front and center on the little platform to give your introductory speech. That way, no eyes could miss you and you think, for one delusionary moment, that you're the cream of the crop. Made a woman my age feel really special. After all, at sixty-eight, three months and four days, and a little *over-the-hill*, I highly doubted there were going to be any young studs falling head over heels in love with me and showering me with their attention.

"Pardon me, ma'am." He gave a brief nod and sat back down again.

I took that as an apology. I could see the look on Merlene's face as she sat in the fourth row from the front. She thought I'd blown my cover for a minute there, but she keeps forgetting that I'm no amateur at protecting my interests. Sure, I sometimes talk a bit too much and gotta put my foot in my mouth afterwards, but my decades of existence give me an excuse.

I could hear Merlene scolding me now:

"Lucille, I've told you time and time again, you must be careful of what you say! No one's gonna understand how an actual blind woman can see the way you do. They won't believe you even if you told them!"

Her words were like a scorched record playing in my brain. She got on my nerves with all her warnings, but I was surely glad I was able to drag her down there to the meeting with me that day.

I tried not to face that guy's direction anymore, even though the dark sunglasses I wore served its purpose of concealing my *blind stare.*

"Thank you, sir," I said. "Well, I guess there's not much left to say about me, except that I used to have a career as a private banker for about twenty years. After that, I retired to spend more time with Donnie, who'd just retired from the Military a year earlier. We spent the next twenty-one years together until he passed away from heart trouble."

Someone else stood up—this time a lady around my age. "If you don't mind my asking…at what point did you lose your eyesight? And how are you possibly able to care for your pet Vanilla?"

When I revisit that part of my life, I tend to get a tad emotional. "It was a little over eight years ago that I developed a rare disease known as Simbalio Flonilia. I know, it sounds like a deadly virus or something, but it's a progressive and rather aggressive deterioration of the retina. They don't know what causes it, but within a year of my diagnosis, I was totally blind. I'm thankful for Donnie because after it happened, he kept me sane. Needless to say, I wasn't handling being blind so well after having been able to see all of my life. Donnie was truly a lifesaver and so was Nilla. She's so smart—she gets me everything I need and she's very protective, despite her little size. I've cared for Nilla ever since she was two months old and I pretty much know where everything is regarding her. Taking care of her is the easy part. Her taking care of me is another story."

Though somewhat hazy, I could see the smiles on many of their faces. The talk of Nilla obviously softened some of their rugged features.

Mrs. Claire Fairweather, the chairperson, came and stood right next to me.

"Lucille, we are happy to welcome you as the newest member of our organization!" She spoke, eagerly. "You have obviously been a productive member of Chadsworth for many years and more importantly, you are a loving mom to your precious little dog, Vanilla. People, let's give her a warm round of applause!"

A gentleman came and helped me to my chair. The fragrance he was wearing reminded me of how much Donnie loved his cologne. Such a fine man, he was. If it were up to him, I wouldn't have worked a day of my married life. It would've been enough for him to see me every day at home just looking pretty and smiling. His engineering job paid well enough, but I loved my career and since it wasn't a stressful one, I didn't feel the need to quit to just sit home and do nothing.

"Thank you, dear," I told the nice, young man.

"My pleasure, Mrs. Pfiffer."

Merlene leaned in as Claire proceeded with the meeting. "I told you—you talk too blasted much!" She whispered. "If you keep up this nonsense, they're gonna take your prized disability checks away from you."

"It'll happen over my dead body, Merlene," I calmly replied.

"Mrs. Pfiffer, I must say it's truly an honor that you've decided to join us here at the Pichton Pet Society," Claire said at the podium. "With your experience as a professional, I'm sure you'll have lots of ideas on how we can raise funds for the continued care of senior pets, stray dogs and abused animals. Your contribution to this group would be greatly appreciated."

After the meeting, she'd caught Merlene and me at the door, as we were about to head for Merlene's Toyota.

"I'm so glad you joined us, Mrs. Pfiffer. My secretary will be in touch with you about our next meeting."

"Thank you, Mrs. Fairweather. I'm honored that you accepted me. After all, animals are most precious. Anything that supports their best interest, I'm fired up for."

"Did you always love animals?" she asked.

I gulped. "Well, if I may be straight with you... I hated them— especially dogs!"

Her hand flew to her chest and a scowl crept over her face. I must have startled her by the revelation.

"It was after Nilla came into our life that I soon found a deep love and appreciation for animals—especially dogs. To me, they're just like precious little children who depend on us adults to take care of them and to show them love, as I quickly learned that they have the biggest heart for their owners."

Fairweather seemed relieved and a wide smile stretched across her face. "Oh, that's so good to know! I was afraid there for a moment that we'd made a terrible mistake by accepting you into our organization!" She laughed it off.

I did a pretend laugh back at her. I may be blind, but I'm not stupid—that woman actually just insulted me to my face!

"I don't know why you want to be a part of that crummy group with those snooty, snobbish, high society creeps anyway!" Merlene remarked after we both got in the car.

I rested my cane beside me. "Because I've been a part of crummy groups for most of my adult life. I don't know anything different."

Merlene gave me a reprimanding look. "It's not funny, Lucille. You dragged me out here to sit with people who, I admit love animals, but they seem to hate humans! I've heard some things about that Fairweather woman that'll make your eyes roll. You know she's a professor at the state college, right?"

"Uh huh."

"Well, I heard she treats the kids who register for her class really badly. She fails most of them every single term. The only ones who pass are the ones who kiss up to her."

"If there's a high failure rate in her class, why would the state keep her on then?" I asked.

"Politics. She got there through politics and is pretty much untouchable. I heard she also was a tyrant to her step-kids. Pretty much ran them all out of the house and practically drove the second fool who married her insane. He actually ended up in the loony bin and when he died, she took everything—not giving his kids a drink of water they can say they'd inherited."

"I blame the husband for that."

"Not when she got him to sign over everything to her in his will when he wasn't in his right mind. The whole thing was contested, but because she was politically connected, she came out on top. After that, she moved on to husband number three. If I knew that woman was the chairperson of this meeting you dragged me out to, I would've waited in the car for you instead of sitting in the same room with her."

We were almost home when Merlene finally stopped talking about Fairweather. You'd think the woman didn't have a life of her own, considering the length of time she focused on this one individual she obviously couldn't stand. I just wanted to get the hell out of that hot car (the two front windows of which couldn't roll down), and get home to my Nilla. She'd be waiting near the door for me for sure.

I wish I was allowed to bring her to the meeting. They claimed they're all about animals, but not one was in that room. I guess I was being unfair since they mentioned that particular Monday meeting was the only one they couldn't bring their pets to. That was the meeting where new members were introduced and important plans for fundraisers were often discussed.

"I'll see you later, Lucille. Going home to do some laundry," Merlene said after pulling up onto my driveway. "Need help getting out?"

"I'm good," I replied.

"How sharp is it now?"

"I can see the outline of your face. Nothing else at the moment. Everything was almost crystal clear in the meeting."

"Yeah. Inopportune time for it to have been crystal clear," Merlene mumbled.

She was used to my *inner vision*, as we call it, going in and out like that. I grabbed hold of my cane and the tip of it hit the ground as I turned to get out of the vehicle. "I can manage just fine. I'm sure it'll come back when it feels like. Thanks for coming out with me."

I smiled as I thought of how much she often sacrificed for me. Ten years my junior, Merlene was a good friend. We had a row almost every day, but we loved one another. She and I were like the typical married couple.

"By the way, I forgot to mention, my tenant Theodore, told me this morning that someone had called about renting the last vacant room."

"Perfect!" Merlene said.

"Said he was coming by this afternoon. What time is it?"

"It's a quarter of five."

I had an idea. "Merlene, he's supposed to show up at five o'clock. You wanna hang around for a few minutes to see what my prospects are? Maybe he's tall, dark and handsome and I may stand a chance."

"I doubt it," she squawked. "Besides, I must get at least a load of laundry done today. If not, I'll likely have to double up tomorrow for as quick as that boy goes through clothes! I tell ya, ever since he met that Delilah, he's changed so much."

"Why don't you leave that boy alone?" I barked. "He's twenty-seven-years-old, for Heaven's sake! Allow him to date whomever the hell he feels like. He's gotta live and learn, you know, and buck his head when need be. You and I went through it and so must he. You surely didn't allow your folks to tell you who you ought to date and who you shouldn't, did you? And furthermore, why do you keep calling Juliet, *Delilah*?"

"Because she's just like that Delilah woman in the Bible; can't be trusted!" Merlene spoke her mind. "And since you asked—why do you call her *Juliet*? Her name's Sabrina."

I sighed. "You know why I call her that."

"I tell ya...she's no Juliet!"

"Anyway, you're gonna wait with me a few minutes while I interview this newcomer or not?" I'd just had enough of Merlene's bickering for one day.

I heard her roll up the two remaining car windows and pull her key out of the ignition. It was one among a ring of keys.

Nilla was right at the front door when I let myself in. I leaned down and scooped up my little princess. She licked my face and I could feel the soft vibration of her wagging tail. Merlene walked in behind me.

"Nilla pilla!" she said, as she plonked down on the sofa. "Why can't you assist

Mommy here with her interview? After all, you've gotta live with the newbie too."

I heard Theodore's footsteps descending the staircase. His was a totally different vibration from Anthony's. Anthony's steps were softer like that of a woman's feet. I had a good look at him a few times and he definitely was *Mister Debonair*. And that desk job he had at the computer company suited him just fine. Theodore was different; he was more hardcore, a blue collar worker at the welding plant, pee sprinkling the toilet seat kinda guy. That was my biggest problem with him – he wasn't all that tidy, especially in the bathroom. But I hadn't kicked him out already because he's got good manners and sort of treats me like I'm his mother. Anthony mostly stays to himself and that's fine with me too.

After I'd sat down, Nilla wiggled constantly to get out of my arms. She didn't like "hands" as much as she preferred dashing all over the place, particularly when her energy level was high. I could tell that was the case at the moment, so I gently let her down on the tiled floor and immediately saw her sprinting through the wide hallway which led into the kitchen, then doubling back into the living room seconds later, and making her way under the sofa. Under there was her favorite spot in the entire house. Often, she stayed in her hut-like habitat for hours at a time.

"Good evening, ladies," Theodore said as he entered the living room. How did the meeting go?"

"It was horrible!" Merlene replied.

"It went fine, Theodore. Beautiful atmosphere; beautiful people," I said.

"She got her fifteen minutes of fame," Merlene snapped. "That's all she cares about. She should've invited *you* to waste a full two hours there instead of me."

Theodore laughed. "Well, I'll be heading out to work. See you later."

"Yeah, later," Merlene replied.

As Theodore opened the door, he met someone standing on the other side. "Oh, I'm sorry. Almost bumped into you," he said.

Theodore went his way and the person stepped inside.

"What're you doing here, David?" Merlene asked.

"I'm here to see Miss Lucille. I'm interested in renting the room."

I could sense Merlene's shock. After all, why would her son who lives with her come to rent a room from me?

Alan Danzabar has been accused of participating in a blatant bank robbery that resulted in the shooting death of a security guard.

All fingers are pointing at Alan by others who have been arrested and ultimately confessed to the crime, but Alan insists that he is innocent.

Will he get off the hook with the help of J. Wilfred & Company, particularly an employee there by the name of Barbara Sandosa who takes it upon herself to dig much deeper to uncover the truth in ways that her boss would never dream of? Or will Alan Danzabar be exposed as a liar and a killer?

Series overview:

Barbara Sandosa, a pastry lover and avid cook, works in her small town's most reputable law firm.

And although she's been hired to do a particular job, she finds herself prying into the private lives of her boss's clients, unbeknownst to them and drags young Harry Buford along for the "rocky" ride. What she uncovers in some cases shocks the innocent minds of those in her community, including her level-headed boss who's being handsomely paid to defend all who have retained his services.

Will Barbara's curiosity literally save the day or will it get her into deep trouble - possibly costing her her job?

FICTION TITLES BY TANYA R. TAYLOR

TANYA-R-TAYLOR.COM

* LUCILLE PFIFFER MYSTERY SERIES
Blind Sight
Blind Escape
Blind Justice
Blind Fury
Blind Flames
Blind Risk
Blind Vacation

INFESTATION: A Small Town Nightmare (The Complete Series)

* THE REAL ILLUSIONS SERIES
Real Illusions: The Awakening
Real Illusions II: REBIRTH
Real Illusions III: BONE OF MY BONE
Real Illusions IV: WAR ZONE

* CORNELIUS SAGA SERIES
Cornelius (Book 1 in the Cornelius saga. *Each book in this series can stand-alone.*)
Cornelius' Revenge (Book 2 in the Cornelius saga)

CARA: Some Children Keep Terrible Secrets (Book 3 in the Cornelius saga)
We See No Evil (Book 4 in the Cornelius saga)
The Contract: Murder in The Bahamas (Book 5 in the Cornelius saga)
The Lost Children of Atlantis (Book 6 in the Cornelius saga)
Death of an Angel (Book 7 in the Cornelius saga)
The Groundskeeper (Book 8 in the Cornelius saga)
Cara: The Beginning - Matilda's Story (Book 9 in the Cornelius saga)
The Disappearing House (Book 10 in the Cornelius saga)
Wicked Little Saints (Book 11 in the Cornelius saga)
A Faint Whisper (Book 12 in the Cornelius saga)
'Til Death Do Us Part (Book 13 in the Cornelius saga)

* THE NICK MYERS SERIES
Hidden Sins Revealed (A Crime Thriller - Nick Myers Series Book 1)
One Dead Politician (Nick Myers Series Book 2)

Haunted Cruise: The Shakedown
The Haunting of MERCI HOSPITAL

10 Minutes before Sleeping

CPSIA information can be obtained
at www.ICGtesting.com
Printed in the USA
LVHW081806071022
730138LV00014B/417